They stood in ~~~~ ~~~~ for a moment, **sizing each other up in some kind** **of face-off.**

With the bed behind her, and his masculine frame leaning against the doorjamb, arms crossed in a tense yet sexy pose…

Well, he wasn't exactly blocking her escape route, but that was the problem. Megan didn't feel like running off, and she really ought to. Because what she found most troubling was the way her heart rate was zipping along at an arousing pace, setting her hormones on high alert and sending her thoughts drifting in a direction they had no business veering.

Peyton Johnson was a handsome man, and while he wore denim and boots, something about him flashed City Boy in neon lights.

Still, she fou~~~~ ~~~~eing "attracted" to ~~~~g as being intereste~~~~ was not interested.

Return to Brighton Valley:
Who says you can't go home again?

THE BACHELOR'S
BRIGHTON
VALLEY BRIDE

BY
JUDY DUARTE

MILLS & BOON

Published in Great Britain 2014
by Mills & Boon, an imprint of Harlequin (UK) Limited,
Eton House, 18-24 Paradise Road, Richmond, Surrey, TW9 1SR

© 2014 Judy Duarte

ISBN: 978-0-263-91301-9

23-0714

Harlequin (UK) Limited's policy is to use papers that are natural, renewable and recyclable products and made from wood grown in sustainable forests. The logging and manufacturing processes conform to the legal environmental regulations of the country of origin.

Printed and bound in Spain
by Blackprint CPI, Barcelona

Judy Duarte always knew there was a book inside her, but since English was her least favorite subject in school, she never considered herself a writer. An avid reader who enjoys a happy ending, Judy couldn't shake the dream of creating a book of her own.

Her dream became a reality in March 2002, when Mills & Boon released her first book, *Cowboy Courage*. Since then she has published more than twenty novels. Her stories have touched the hearts of readers around the world. And in July 2005 Judy won a prestigious Readers' Choice Award for *The Rich Man's Son*.

Judy makes her home near the beach in Southern California. When she's not cooped up in her writing cave, she's spending time with her somewhat enormous but delightfully close family.

To Teresa Carpenter and Jill Limber,
who helped me plot the details of
Clay and Megan's story during a girls' getaway
and gabfest in Orange County. If you ever want
to have another slumber party, ladies, count me in!

Chapter One

For most people, returning to their roots brought on a warm sense of nostalgia—but that wasn't the case for Clay Jenkins.

As he sat in a nondescript SUV on the tree-shaded main drag of Brighton Valley, just three buildings down from the old computer repair shop where he'd first gone to work nine years ago, he was reminded of the life he'd eagerly left behind and had tried so hard to forget.

He could have hired someone else to come in and fix his flagship store, but this was where his new life had actually started.

Hank Lazaro, his friend and mentor, had gotten him his first job there. As a result, the time he'd spent here on the weekends and after school had kept him out of trouble—and it had taught him a lot about business and honesty and hard work. It was here that he'd met the financial backer who'd helped him market the computer software program that had made him a multimillionaire before he hit the ripe old age of twenty.

Clay knew he shouldn't attach so much emotional significance to the quaint old building, especially in a small Texas town that, as a teenager, he couldn't wait to escape. But when he'd seen the last quarterly reports and realized that a corporate rep from Geekon Enterprises would have to step in and turn the store around before it went down the tubes…well, the task had become personal, and he knew he was the only one he would allow to do it.

He got out of the vehicle he'd rented at the executive airport in Houston, where he'd arrived in his private jet, and sucked in a deep breath of country air. As he caught the aroma coming from Caroline's Diner, his stomach growled, reminding him he hadn't eaten anything but a bagel at the Silicon Valley office earlier this morning.

No one made a better meal than Caroline, at least when it came to down-home cooking like chicken-fried steak, meat loaf, pork chops and the like. He could practically recite her menu from memory—unless she'd changed it. But something told him she'd never do that.

When he'd worked here, he'd eaten lunch at Caroline's every day, filling up on her daily special—no matter what it was. Of course, he stuck to a healthy diet now, but that didn't mean he wouldn't slip off to the diner the first chance he got—for old times' sake.

Clay removed his dark-tinted sunglasses, doubting he'd need them to hide his identity from any of the locals who might remember him. He no longer looked like the nerdy, undeveloped teenager who'd first got his start working as a computer repair technician at Ralph's Electronics.

Seven years ago, when Ralph died, Clay purchased the business from his widow for ten times its value and made it part of the Zorba the Geek chain, a subsidiary of Geekon Enterprises, which also owned GeekMart, a chain of computer stores that had launched the innovative Geekon line of computers.

Ralph had hired Don Carpenter six months earlier, so Clay had let him continue to manage the Brighton Valley repair shop. Then he'd flown back to Silicon Valley, leaving the sad memories and the small town behind. Or so he'd thought.

But here he was, dressed in a pair of khaki slacks and a black polo shirt, hoping he looked as though he belonged in the bucolic world he'd long since outgrown.

He'd much rather be back in California, wearing one of his many custom-made suits, going out on the town this evening. But when his executive assistant had given him that requested update on the Brighton Valley store and he'd seen that Don Carpenter hadn't turned in his yearly sales-and-service report, Clay had known something wasn't right.

He hated to think that someone was embezzling funds or doing something otherwise illegal in one of his companies, but with hundreds of shops operating around the world, it wouldn't be the first time.

While he could hire someone else to go in and find the cause—or the culprit—he was determined to handle this situation himself, even if that meant he had to go undercover to do it.

And that shouldn't be difficult. Clay had been too busy to talk to Don in person when he'd purchased the store. Instead, all their conversations had taken place over the phone and via email.

Clay had also grown up in nearby Wexler, so not too many people in Brighton Valley knew him. And just in case anyone followed the business magazines, which he doubted in a one-horse town like this, he'd shaved off his trendy beard, cut his stylish shoulder-length hair, opted for a pair of contacts instead of his black-framed glasses, and traded in his suits and Italian loafers for a more casual look. So he felt confident that his identity was safe.

For that reason, as he stepped onto the sidewalk, feeling a bit like Clark Kent, he held on to his self-assured swagger, unwilling to give up everything he'd worked so hard to perfect.

As he made his way down the shady street, he paused in front of the hardware store and gazed at some of the same familiar items showcased for sale. In fact, not much in Brighton Valley had changed since he used to ride his secondhand bike to work every afternoon and chain it up to the parking meter out front.

On the other hand, Clay had morphed into an entirely new being. At twenty-six, he was no longer the scrawny kid who'd had to worry about using a lock to secure that same bike so the football jocks wouldn't steal it, paint it pink and toss it up into the branches of the elm tree that grew in front of the gym.

In fact, with the kind of money and power that he could now wield, nobody would ever mess with him again.

That is, if they knew who he really was.

But Clay didn't want them to know. At least, not yet.

He turned and made his way to the once-familiar shop and let himself in.

The jingling of the bell on the door signaled his entrance, and he took a moment to scan the shelves of new and refurbished computers for sale, as well as the wooden counter that ran the length of the small reception area and blocked the entrance to the workstations in the rear of the shop.

He sucked in a breath and caught the whiff of…cinnamon and…sugar?

Zorba the Geek hardly smelled like dust and toner any longer. Why was that? And where was everyone? Hadn't they heard the ringing when he came in?

When Clay worked here, he used to drop everything he was doing to greet whoever entered the store. The customer service had certainly gone downhill, which could account for some of the store's trouble.

"Hello," he called out, hoping to alert someone in back to his arrival.

Footsteps sounded, and an attractive redhead came out, the telephone to her ear. She wore a pair of snug jeans and a blue tank shirt that wasn't what he'd call revealing, but certainly caressed her curves

When she spotted him, she held up a slender nail-polished finger, indicating she'd be with him in a moment.

Her auburn brows were knit tightly above big, round eyes the same color as the caramel-flavored coffee his executive assistant brought him from Starbucks every morning.

Maybe it was due to the fact that he was growing hungrier by the minute—or to the sweet scent of sugar and cinnamon that had set his taste buds on edge—but damn if those big brown eyes didn't make him crave a taste of caramel.

That is, until the pretty redhead shot him a stressed-out glance that brought him back to reality.

"He's never done this before," she told the caller. "Are you sure it was him?"

Clay suspected she was trying to appease a customer who was unhappy with their service.

"Uh-huh." She bit down on her bottom lip. "What about the other boy? Did he say that Tyler started it?"

Now, *that* didn't sound like a business-related conversation. Was she on a personal call? With a customer standing in front of her, waiting for assistance?

Okay, so technically, Clay *wasn't* a customer, but she didn't know that.

In spite of her pretty brown eyes and enough curves to inspire a supermodel to go out and eat a cheeseburger and fries, Clay's annoyance rose to the point that he was having a difficult time remaining quiet.

No wonder the store was in trouble. Don had hired an employee who couldn't be bothered to put business ahead of her personal life.

"I'm sure this is just a onetime thing, Mrs. Paxton. Tell Tyler I'll be there as soon as I can." The redhead ended the call and, with the phone still in her hand, rubbed at her temples as if trying to massage the obvious stress out of her brain.

Then she reached under the wooden counter and pulled out a plate of cookies. "I'm so sorry. That was my son's school and… Can I offer you a snickerdoodle? I made them this morning."

So that was what was responsible for the sweet

cinnamon-laced scent that had been taunting him since he'd walked in the door.

But serving cookies to the customers? He was pretty sure *that* concept hadn't been introduced at the last public-relations focus-group session. Maybe the Brighton Valley branch didn't get the memo that they were in a computer repair shop, not a bakery.

Yet he wasn't going to come in with corporate guns blazing and start nitpicking every little thing the store was obviously doing wrong. Not to mention, he was having some pretty heavy hunger pangs. And while he tried to be health conscious, especially in recent years, he'd never been able to turn down sweets.

He picked up a cookie and asked, "Is Don Carpenter in?"

"I'm sorry, but he's out for the rest of the afternoon. Is there something I can do for you?"

"I'm Peyton Johnson. The Houston office sent me down to help you get your new accounting system up and running. Don was expecting me."

Clay took a quick bite, and when the cookie melted in his mouth, he closed his eyes for a moment, savoring the sweet taste. Then he quickly swallowed, realizing that he was still waiting for the redhead to explain who she was.

Apparently, he'd have to wait longer, because the phone in her hand rang again and she barely glanced at the display screen before taking the call, ignoring him for a second time.

She did, however, give him the just-a-minute signal before answering, "Yes?"

She might be beautiful—and that annoying finger

made a damn fine cookie—but he didn't like being asked to wait.

One thing was certain, though. She had no idea who he really was, because no one put Clayton Jenkins on hold.

"Doesn't the nurse have an ice pack?" she asked the caller.

Clay took another bite of the cookie and listened to the one-sided conversation, trying to figure out what was more important than this woman's future employment—which was growing shakier by the second.

"Well, Mrs. Paxton, I'm a bit more concerned with my son getting beat up by Conner Doyle, who I believe is a bully, than I am about Conner having to rewrite his essay on the rain-forest biome because he didn't save the document in the computer lab."

Bully? The once-delicious cookie turned to chalk in Clay's mouth. It hadn't been that long ago that a certain football jock had made his adolescent life hell.

"Well, if the document was saved, then…uh…Well, wasn't it password protected?…Uh-huh…I see." After a beat, she said, "I'm sure Tyler didn't hack into anything."

Hack? Now, that word sparked a rather magical memory. Years ago, Clay had used his skill in technology to fight back against the bigger and tougher kids at school, and it had worked like a charm.

"Suspended? Don't you think that's a little extreme?"

It sounded like the boy—her son—was in trouble.

"Is Conner being suspended, too?" Those brown eyes widened, and she tightened her grip on the receiver. "What do you mean, 'not at this time'? Actually, don't answer that. Don't do anything. I'll be right there."

After disconnecting the call, she waved at Clay, indicating that he should follow her toward the back office.

People didn't order Clay to do anything, and while every fiber in his being wanted to balk, he trailed behind her as she strode to a desk and yanked open the lower drawer.

She appeared to be in full mama-tigress mode, preparing to protect her cub. Clay couldn't help but be a bit envious of the lucky kid. His own mother had never gone to battle for him. Of course, he couldn't hold that against her. She'd had her own struggles to deal with, and more often than not, Clay had needed to take care of her.

"Listen, Mr…" The redhead paused and glanced up from where she'd stooped over, her eyes wide, her lips parted.

Apparently, she hadn't paid a bit of attention when he'd told her his name.

"Johnson," he said, repeating the alias he'd come up with. "Peyton Johnson. And you're . . . ?"

"Megan Adams." She reached for a black purse that had seen better days, then kicked the desk drawer shut. "I'm so sorry to do this to you, Mr. Johnson. But since you work for Zorba's anyway, would you mind covering the shop for me for a couple of minutes? I have to run to the middle school. It's just down the street, so I'll be right back."

Her keys were in her hand and she was heading out the back door before Clay could voice either an objection or an agreement.

As he heard a car backing out of the parking spot in the alley, he turned to look at the cluttered desk piled with coffee-stained work invoices and an open green ledger.

While stunned and annoyed that the woman had just left him in the back office with all the pricey equipment and access to confidential business information, he decided not to look a gift horse in the mouth. Instead he'd take the opportunity to get a peek at what was really going on with the store, although he had a pretty good idea already.

He still didn't know anything about the woman other than her name, but if her behavior at the front counter and the disarray of this desk were any indication, he knew she didn't have the work ethic that Geekon Enterprises expected from those on their payroll.

And it didn't matter how sultry her eyes were—or that his hands itched to touch her abundant red hair.

Nor did it matter that she made a damn good cookie.

Business came first, and Clay had to do what was best for the store—even if that meant firing the first employee he'd met.

Megan could have died when the handsome dark-haired stranger had come into the shop and introduced himself as the accounting specialist the corporate office had sent to get their store in order—or to spy on them, depending on how you wanted to look at things.

The truth was, the shop desperately needed his help. But they didn't need him reporting back to corporate and getting her and her boss fired.

When Don Carpenter first hired Megan to help out in the store a few months back, the job had been a godsend. And despite the fact that she knew very little about computers—and not much more about bookkeeping—

it hadn't taken long for her to realize the store was in big trouble.

Don was a wonderful older man, a kindhearted boss and a loving husband, but she feared that his worry about his wife had caused him to become scattered lately. He'd also been so busy looking after her and taking her to appointments that he'd gotten behind on his work. And to top it all off, he was intent upon doing things the "old way" and had been resistant to converting to a new, electronic accounting system.

Megan tried to do what she could to help, but the store was going under, and she wasn't sure if she could turn things around on her own. Sadly, poor Don couldn't afford to lose his job right now, especially with his wife still undergoing chemotherapy. So Megan had brought in Tyler to assist him with some of the easier repair work. And while her twelve-year-old son had been helpful at times, he also causing her more stress lately.

She glanced at the sulky boy hunched into the front seat beside her. His lip was split, and he hadn't said a word since she'd blasted into his principal's office and exchanged some heated words with the woman—and with Conner Doyle's parents.

She hated being a tattletale or fighting Tyler's battles for him, but it was unfair for her son to get suspended for retaliating the only way he knew how.

Conner had been picking on Tyler ever since they'd moved to Brighton Valley last summer, and the bullying had only gotten worse. She'd sensed a change in her son during the school year. The sweet, fun-loving boy had grown quieter each day, withdrawing into books and technology and other solitary activities. It concerned her because it was something she couldn't relate to, and she feared losing the connection they'd always had.

She stole another glance at Tyler, noting his red hair, his thin frame. In many ways, he'd taken after her side of the family in looks. She had no idea where he'd inherited his amazing intellect. She'd never been a great student, and her ex-husband, Todd Redding, who'd been athletic and quick on his feet, had excelled far better on the football field than he had in the classroom.

To make matters worse—and no doubt compounding what Tyler might be going through now—Todd had never wanted much to do with his nonathletic, bookish son, even before he'd abandoned the family. And that was one reason Megan had taken back her maiden name when they were divorced. Another was to distance herself from the terrible financial situation Todd had left her in.

When she stopped at the intersection near the town square, she reached over and tousled her son's red hair. "I love you no matter what, Ty. And I want you to know that when you're ready to talk about what happened, I'll be here to listen."

He didn't respond, yet he didn't move away from her caressing hand, either.

She pulled her old Civic into the parking spot in the back alley behind Zorba's and shut off the ignition, her thoughts still desperately groping for a solution. And while she wasn't sure what to do to help her son, she couldn't very well leave Mr. Johnson alone to poke around the store more than she already had. But she'd had no other choice. Had he not been there, she would have locked up and left an "out to lunch" sign on the front door.

Megan glanced at her reflection in the rearview mirror, wishing she had some lip gloss and mascara.

And why was that? She hadn't gone out of her way to look attractive for anyone since before her divorce. Of course, there'd never been any extra money for frivolities like makeup or new clothes. Besides, the last thing she needed was for a man to show any interest in her.

So why was she now so concerned with how she looked for Mr. Big-Shot Accountant?

"Did Mr. Carpenter leave that MacBook for me to adjust?" Tyler asked as he hopped out of the car and headed toward the back entrance.

Oh, no! She'd forgotten to tell Tyler that Mr. Johnson was here. And for that reason, he couldn't do any more of the repairs—at least, not during business hours.

She unlatched her seat belt and hustled out of the car, trying to intercept the boy before he made it inside.

"Whoa," Tyler said before she could stop him. "Who are you?"

Mr. Johnson, who'd been seated at Don Carpenter's desk, spun the chair toward the door as they entered.

Had he gotten better-looking while she'd been gone? Or had she just been too distracted on the phone to notice that his eyes were an amazing shade of blue, that he had a square-cut jaw, that his lips were full and sensuous?

"I'm Peyton Johnson." He stood and extended his hand to Tyler. "I work for Zorba the Geek."

While Megan hadn't paid too much attention to his facial features before, she definitely noted them now, especially the way his blue eyes narrowed in on her as he said, "And now will somebody be so kind as to tell me who you two are?"

Oh, no. Hadn't she introduced herself when he'd arrived? Her memory replayed the sequence of events between when he'd entered the shop and when she'd dashed out. As the conversation, at least most of it, played back to her, she could have sworn she'd told him her name. But maybe she hadn't.

"I'm so sorry. I'm Megan Adams. I help Mr. Carpenter here in the back office. This is my son, Tyler. He got in trouble at school today, and I'm afraid dealing with all of that made me a little flustered. I'm not normally like this."

Peyton's intent stare sent a nervous flutter through her, threatening to scatter her thoughts to the winds, so she averted her eyes from his face, her gaze slipping down to the open black collar that exposed a sliver of dark chest hair.

"So," Mr. Johnson said, reining in her thoughts from the slight sexual diversion they'd taken, "what exactly do you do here at Zorba the Geek? Are you a computer tech?"

"Ha!" Laughter came from the boy behind her, but before she could turn and shush him, he added, "Mom wouldn't know a gigabyte from an integrated circuit."

Peyton's brows rose, and he looked over Megan's head, which wasn't all that hard for him to do, since she stood only five foot two. "And you do?"

"Of course I do. Take this Geekon hard drive right here." Tyler pointed to one of the black boxes disassembled on an empty workstation against the wall. "This model uses a digital integrated circuit." He went on to talk about logic gates and signals and values of ones and zeroes, all of which went over Megan's head. "See, all the Geekon series use digital ICs."

"What do you think of the Geekon series?" Peyton asked the usually quiet boy, who hadn't said more than three sentences to her all week.

Tyler perked up and launched into a full discourse on the uses of microprocessors and transistors and everything else that caused Megan to tune him out.

"So basically," Tyler said, "straight out of the box, Geekon computers are the best you can buy. But they're not the best that can be made."

"*Tyler,* Mr. Johnson works for Zorba the Geek, which is part of Geekon Enterprises, *remember?*" Megan left the rest unsaid, hoping that her normally introverted son knew better than to insult the product that was responsible for providing her paycheck.

The boy lovingly patted the black hard drive on the table. "Then I'm sure Mr. Johnson would want to see what I can do with this baby to make it run even better."

Oh, jeez.

"You know what, Tyler? I certainly would like to see that. But I'm here from the accounting department. Maybe when I get finished here, I can call some buddies who run the manufacturing department and set you up with someone who designs this stuff for a living."

"Sweet!"

Well, at least one person was excited about Mr. Johnson being there.

When Peyton returned to Mr. Carpenter's desk, he looked at it as if he wanted to pick up the whole thing, mounds of paperwork and all, and throw it in the Dumpster out back.

Shoot. Who could blame him? Whenever Megan tried to tackle the piles of old invoices that had been stacked up months before she'd even started working here, she felt like tossing it all out herself. She didn't even know where to start sorting out the jumbled mess.

"I don't even know where to start," Peyton said.

Great, he was an accountant *and* a mind reader.

"Things have gotten a wee bit backed up since Mrs. Carpenter got sick," she admitted.

Of course, in a matter of days—maybe even hours—Mr. Johnson was going to figure it out on his own. But in the meantime, it wouldn't hurt to try and make the corporate lapdog see that they were all doing their best and that none of them should lose their jobs.

"Do you have a game plan for how long you'll be in town?" she asked, hoping he'd say it would be for only a few hours.

"As long as it takes. The corporate office got me a room at the Night Owl."

The motel was right off the highway and near the Stagecoach Inn, a local honky-tonk. Neither seemed to be the kind of place that would appeal to a man like Peyton Johnson, although that was mere speculation on her part—and quite frankly, it was none of her business or her concern.

"Too bad you can't stay in the apartment upstairs," Tyler said. "It would make it a lot closer for you."

The boy's suggestion took the wind right out of her, making it impossible to respond, let alone object.

"It's got a bed and stuff up there," Tyler added. "And it's also got a TV and a kitchen."

"Is it vacant?" Peyton asked.

"Yeah," Tyler said.

Megan's stomach tightened. How did she go about keeping the boy quiet? "The company has made arrangements for Mr. Johnson to stay at a motel, Tyler. I'm sure they've already made a deposit. And if not, there's probably a cancellation fee. Besides, there's not much to do in downtown Brighton Valley in the evenings. But at the Night Owl, he'd be so much closer to Wexler and all the bigger-city amenities he's probably used to."

She offered a smile, hoping she'd squelched her son's impromptu suggestion before Peyton got any ideas. It was bad enough that he was going to be spending the next day or so looking over their old accounting system and seeing how bad things had gotten. But having him spending nights here, too?

"You know," Peyton said, "I think I'll give the office a call. It would be a lot more convenient to just stay here. And if I can get my job done sooner, I'll be saving the company money in the long run. They'll surely see the savings there."

As Peyton pulled out his cell phone and prepared to dial, Megan's heart sank. She'd hoped that she could lock him out of the shop each evening, knowing that she'd be present whenever he uncovered the problems facing the store—and that she could explain and maybe soften the blow.

But how could she do that if he had access to the office when she wasn't around to protect Mr. Carpenter?

She wanted to snatch the cell phone out of his hands, but she'd been raised better than that. So she stood there pretending to smile gamely, feeling absolutely powerless and at her wit's end as she shot a glance at the one man who had the ability to turn her life upside down once again.

It had taken her three long years after the divorce to put her life back to rights again, and she was finally seeing some light at the end of a very dark financial tunnel. Then in walked Peyton Johnson, who had the ability to jerk the rug out from under her and shake up all she'd fought so hard to build.

But she was up for the challenge. There was no way she'd stand by and let another man dash her dreams again without putting up a fight.

Chapter Two

Clay pulled out his cell and called Zoe, his executive assistant, who knew where he was and what he was up to.

"This is Peyton Johnson. I'm at the Brighton Valley store, and it's come to my attention that there's an apartment over the shop. I'm not sure how that will pencil out for the corporate bean counters, but it would sure be more convenient if I could just stay there. That motel you reserved for me is clear across town."

"You own the building," Zoe told Clay. "I don't have to clear anything—"

"You've got that right, ma'am. So would you mind checking into that for me?"

"I...uh..." Zoe paused. "So this phone call is just for show?"

"Yes, it is."

"And all I'm really supposed to do is listen while you speak?"

"That would be the case. Yes."

"Very clever. I'll have to add an extra line to my job description. The executive assistant must be bilingual in both English and in reading the boss's cryptic telephone conversations."

"Something tells me that could come in handy, especially while I'm in Brighton Valley."

"Then I'm on it. Looks like you're in luck, Clay— I mean Peyton. I can assure you, or rather everyone at the Brighton Valley store, that corporate will approve of anything you suggest."

"It certainly would be in their best interests to do so." Clay smiled. "Thanks, Zoe. Then I'll just wait for you to check into that. How soon do you think you can call back?"

"Would five minutes be a believable response time?"

"That works for me."

"All right, then. You got it, boss. Clock is ticking."

Before Clay could hang up, he spotted Megan pushing her son away from the computer workstation and shoving the worn green backpack into his arms. Then she pointed at the counter in the front of the shop.

Clay placed the cell phone back in his pocket as she muttered something that sounded like, "Not while he's here, you're not."

Tyler looked at Clay, then shuffled his thin-framed adolescent body in the direction his mother was pointing.

So what wasn't Megan allowing her son to do while "Peyton Johnson"—or rather, a corporate rep—was here?

When Clay glanced at Megan, she flashed a smile at him. It was a pleasant smile, but it seemed a bit forced.

What made her so uneasy?

"Why don't I show you around the shop?" she asked.

Clay didn't need a tour. He'd had the run of the place since he was sixteen. He was also the owner of the building. But, of course, he couldn't let on about that.

"Sure. Let's get started." The sooner he got this mess squared away, the sooner he could get the heck out of Brighton Valley. And this time, he'd leave it behind for good.

"You saw the front desk when you came in," she said. "We also have our refurbished computers and some new Geekon models for sale up there. We don't really keep a lot of cash in the store, just enough to make change for the customers. We take credit cards, too, but you probably won't be dealing with any of that."

She must have forgotten that he would have had to deal with all of that if a customer had actually come into the shop when she'd abandoned him to get her son an hour ago. But before either of them could comment, the bell on the door jangled, and an actual customer did walk in.

Or stomped in was more like it, a laptop tucked under his arm, a grimace on his face. "Where's Don? He was supposed to have fixed this darn computer, and I waited nigh on three weeks for it. He finally called me yesterday and told me I could pick it up, so I did. But the fool thing still isn't working right."

Riley McLaughlin, a rather crotchety fellow who'd bought the refurbished machine from Ralph back when Clay used to work here, set the outdated laptop on the counter. "This is the third trip to town I've had to make, and I still can't get online or send an email. How can you folks run a business if a customer can't get any satisfaction?"

"Don isn't here right now," Megan said, "but if you want to leave the laptop here, I'll have him take another look at it."

"And then what?" Riley clucked his tongue. "I'll have to wait another three weeks to get it back?"

"I promise to make sure he looks at it as soon as he gets into the shop. It'll be a high priority." Megan reached under the counter and pulled out the plate of cookies. "Here, try one of my snickerdoodles. I made them this morning."

Riley knit his bushy gray brows together, then glanced at the sweet treats, grumbling as he did. Yet he took one of them and bit into it.

"Let me take a look at that for you," Clay said. "But in the meantime, we just happen to have one of the new Geekon laptops here. Why don't you take it home and give it a try. The corporate office is offering a special deal on this particular model, and there's a ten-day free trial period."

Riley, who was chomping away on Megan's cookie, turned and studied Clay.

For a moment, Clay feared the guy might have recognized him. That is, until Riley asked, "Who are you?"

"Peyton Johnson. I work out of the Houston office."

Riley's scowl faded, and he let out a little humph. "I always did like free trials. But how much do those new laptops cost?"

"From what I understand, if you like the product and are willing to talk up Zorba the Geek, as well as Geekon computers, you can buy it for a a hundred dollars."

Clay reached for the box on the shelf that contained a new Geekon Blast, knowing that price was an unheard of bargain—even for a fellow who was as close to his nickels as Riley was. And it would certainly work a lot better at placating an angry customer than a couple of cookies—no matter how good they were.

At that moment, Clay's smartphone rang—no doubt Zoe calling him back as requested—so he pulled it from his pocket to take the call.

"Are you sure about that discount and offer?" Megan whispered to him before he could answer the phone. "You must be mistaken. A hundred dollars is a ninety-percent savings off the retail price."

He lifted his ringing cell. "Do you want to ask the Houston office about that promotional sale?"

She studied him, those pretty brown eyes darting back and forth as if trying to assess his honesty.

Clay tossed her a crooked grin, then answered the call. "Peyton Johnson."

"Hey, boss. This is your wake-up call—or rather, your apartment's-in-the-bag call."

"Nice. Thanks, Zoe. And while I have you on the phone, can you please talk to Megan, who works here at the Brighton Valley store? I told her all about that hundred-dollar special that the marketing department is running on the Geekon Blast laptop. And she didn't believe me." He handed his phone to Megan, confident Zoe would assure her that she could believe anything Clay—or rather, "Peyton"—had told her, even though Zoe had no knowledge of the phony sale he'd just concocted for Riley's benefit.

As Megan reached for Clay's cell, her fingers brushed his, sparking a warm, feathery rush of heat up his arm. For a moment, their gazes met, and he realized she'd felt something, too.

Then she averted her gaze and spoke into the phone. "Hello?" She listened for a moment or two, then said, "Okay. It's just that it sounded way too good to be true, if you know what I mean. Goodness, if those things only cost a hundred dollars, I'd like one, too."

Again she listened to whatever Zoe was telling her. Then she nodded and handed the phone back to Clay. After thanking Zoe, he ended the call.

"Satisfied?" he asked.

"I guess so. She said you were in that last marketing meeting, and that you're never wrong when it comes to sales and special prices. So she said I could rest assured that the offer was spot-on."

Clay tossed her a grin.

Megan added, "She also said that she'd like one of the Geekon Blast models, too. Her nephew is having a birthday next week and would love a laptop. She's thrilled to know that she can afford to buy him one— thanks to that special price."

"Smart gal, that Zoe. She's always been one to jump on a good deal." Clay would have to tell his executive assistant not to spread the word about the sale. And that it was a onetime deal that would last only until the end of the day.

"So what do you say?" Clay asked, turning back to Riley. "Will you leave your old laptop with me and take this new baby for a test run?"

"You got a deal," Riley said. Then he took the box off the counter, tucked it under his arm and headed out the door.

"I guess a new laptop worked even better at sweetening his mood than my cookies did," Megan said.

"How many customer complaints do you get these days?" Clay asked.

She bit down on her bottom lip. "A few, I guess. Mostly because Don has gotten a little backlogged."

Clay suspected that was an understatement. But he'd find out the truth soon enough.

"Come on," she said, "I'll finish giving you that tour of the shop."

She led him back to the work area, which was three times the size of the front part of the store. Yet it seemed a lot smaller than Clay remembered. Maybe that was because it wasn't just the shelves that were stacked with various new and used computers and laptops. The floors were so cluttered with machines that they'd had to make walkways to get around them.

"This is where Don works," Megan said, indicating the old desk Ralph Weston used to keep as clean as a whistle. Only now the stacks of paper and other stuff made it impossible to see the once-glossy wood grain Ralph used to polish every Saturday afternoon.

Clay followed along as she talked and pointed, but each time she moved or brushed past him, her lavender scent taunted him, causing him to lose focus on what she was saying.

But it certainly didn't cause him to lose his focus on the way her jeans hugged every inch of her curvy bottom—unlike that willowy, reed-thin model he'd dated last. To be honest, he actually found Megan's womanly figure more appealing.

She grabbed a stack of papers off a ledger and shoved them into a bin on top of one of the old green filing cabinets. "I'm in the process of developing a new invoice system that will be easier to manage."

He knew he should be paying a lot more attention to what she was saying and pointing out, even though not a stick of furniture or shelf or cabinet had changed in the ten-plus years since he'd worked here. But he couldn't stop wanting to know more about her.

And less about the new system she'd been trying to explain.

"And that's about the size of it," she said as she ended her small circling tour at the foot of the stairway that led to the second floor. "And up there is the apartment Tyler was talking about, although I suspect you'd be much more comfortable at the Night Owl. Like I said, it's closer to Wexler. And it's right by the Stagecoach Inn, in case you wanted to grab some beers or go dancing or something after work."

"Is that an invitation?" The minute the words rolled off his tongue, he could have kicked himself.

Why in the hell had he asked her that? He'd grown accustomed to women hitting on him, but even a former geek knew Megan was just being friendly and not flirting. Yet the longer he'd watched her bouncing around the store giving him a peppy, upbeat tour, like one of the cheerleaders back at Washington High in Wexler, the more he'd found himself slipping into nerd mode.

"Oh, no. I don't go out on…" A blush spread up the neckline of her shirt, and she averted her sexy brown eyes. "I mean, I don't go out dancing or anything like that. I'm a mom. I have Tyler and Lisa and… That reminds me." She paused and glanced at her watch. "I'm sorry, but since I don't normally work on Wednesdays, I don't have a sitter lined up today. So I have to pick up my daughter. Do you mind watching the store for me again?"

Before, he could answer, the beautiful redhead was out the door like a shot. Just like she'd done the first time he'd seen her.

Clay looked at the stairs leading up to the apartment and wished her tour had continued to the intimate living space above.

Maybe her running out was for the best, because he had no business allowing himself to be distracted. His time in Brighton Valley was limited, and he didn't plan to stay any longer than absolutely necessary.

Hopefully, Don Carpenter would be back soon, because Clay didn't know how he was going to be able to work with the woman without a chaperone.

At the sound of a pencil tapping, he realized they hadn't even been alone now. Megan's son was sitting at the front counter staring at the computers lining the wall instead of writing in his school workbook.

So not only had she left him to look after the store, now she'd left him to babysit her son, too.

Megan Adams might be sexy as hell, but she had to be the most irresponsible employee he'd ever had. And he had a feeling she'd be the first one at the Brighton Valley store that he'd have to let go.

Peyton Johnson couldn't have come at a worse time. And he probably couldn't be any more annoyed at Megan than he was now.

When she'd grabbed her purse a second time and practically run from the shop yet again, he'd merely gaped at her. But she'd had a pretty good idea of what he'd been thinking.

Still, with Don away from the shop, what other option did she have? She couldn't very well leave her second grader at school.

As she turned into the alley that ran behind the shops lining Main Street, Megan glanced into the rearview mirror and caught her daughter's eye. "Lisa, change out of your cleats before we go inside and put on your shoes. You know how hard it is to get all that mud and grass out of the shop's carpet."

"Aw, Mom." The seven-year-old insisted upon wearing her soccer uniform everywhere, even to school. "Then can I go barefoot? My coach said lots of athletes practice without shoes to toughen their feet up. And I want *my* feet to be tough."

Megan hadn't had a chance to vacuum the floor yet, and no telling what small screw or piece of wire might end up in her daughter's foot. All she needed was for Mr. Johnson to think she was violating some safety regulation on top of everything else. "Never mind. Just stomp your shoes before we go inside."

It was bad enough she had both her kids at work with her this afternoon, but with her mom and Ted on their dream vacation of a yearlong RV trip across America, Megan was left without many childcare options until summer camp started at the Wexler YMCA next week.

She held the door open for her blonde daughter, who'd once again left her backpack in the car—no doubt on purpose. "After you meet Mr. Johnson, the new worker I told you about, you need to go back to the car and get your homework. You have to practice your spelling tonight. It's the last test of the year."

Lisa rolled her eyes, transporting Megan back to a time when she used to do the same thing to her own mother. Oh, how she'd hated spelling. And reading. And any other kind of schoolwork that had to do with written words that seemed to jump all over the page.

She really couldn't blame her daughter, who'd inherited the same learning disabilities she'd struggled with in school.

"Why do I even need to learn how to spell all those boring words anyway? Soccer players only need to know how to run fast and kick the ball."

As they entered the back door to the shop, Peyton turned from where he stood perusing the ever-increasing number of backlogged computers that lined the shelves. "Even Mia Hamm had to learn how to spell," Peyton told Lisa.

Megan's stomach nose-dived, and the dull headache that had begun when Tyler's school had first called her this afternoon sharpened. Not only had Peyton heard Lisa's complaint, but he'd actually responded to her.

Great. The man had been in the shop for all of thirty minutes, and he could make a slew of assumptions about her parenting skills. And they hadn't even talked about the problems facing the store—the computers needing repair and the stacks of old invoices that had yet to be logged.

He probably suspected that Megan's son was a computer hacker and her whining daughter hated to read.

Would he realize that Megan's problems with the kids sometimes caused her to be nearly as scattered as Don?

"Who are *you*?" Lisa asked him.

"Lisa!" Megan really had taught her daughter better manners than that. "This is Mr. Johnson. Remember, I told you about him. He's the man from Geekon

Enterprises who's going to be working at the shop for a while."

"Do you know Mia Hamm?" Lisa asked, zeroing in on her all-time favorite women's soccer player.

"I've actually met her. And she's a good speller. She needed to be in order to read those playbooks."

Lisa's eyes widened, and her lips parted. "You *know* her? *Really?*"

Megan had to admit that she was a bit surprised, too. And when she stole a glance at Peyton, she saw a blush creep onto his cheeks.

Why was that? Was he embarrassed to be caught in a lie? Surely he didn't actually know the woman. Or did he?

He glanced away from her and Lisa, as though he wished he could be anywhere but here in the store with them.

"We're not actually friends," he admitted. "I met her at…a charity event. And the spelling thing. I…uh…read that in a magazine somewhere."

"Mom," Lisa said, "is the car unlocked? I have to go get my backpack."

"It's open," Megan said. Then she watched in amused surprise as her daughter raced outside to get her bag.

Megan glanced at Peyton. She'd found it odd that he'd said anything to Lisa in the first place, but if it caused the girl to voluntarily want to do her schoolwork, well, then she wasn't about to complain.

Her gaze focused in on the accountant who'd probably already taken inventory of the way she ran the back office, as well as the way she handled her children.

"Thank you," she said. "That was brilliant."

"Yeah, well, even geeks can relate to sports fanatics sometimes."

A geek? That might be true of some accountants, but there was nothing geeky about Peyton Johnson. He looked as though he'd be more comfortable running track or fielding line drives than adding up columns and running spreadsheets behind some sedentary computer. But Megan wasn't about to say as much.

"It's not always Bring Your Kids to Work Day around here," she said.

Okay, that wasn't exactly true, but Don had left Megan with no other choice if she wanted to keep her health insurance and the extra pay. This was supposed to be a part-time job, but given how often she had to cover for the poor man, she had to come into the shop much more frequently than either of them had planned.

When she realized that Peyton wasn't going to comment, she continued, "But I'm a single mother, and with Tyler having trouble at school today…" She trailed off, cringing as she heard herself play the deserted-mom card. She didn't want anyone cutting her any breaks just because she'd been too stupid to resist Todd Redding's charms.

When she realized Peyton still had yet to respond to anything she'd said, her head began to throb. So she removed the rubber band, releasing her long hair from its high ponytail, and massaged her scalp, trying to ease the ache.

She shook her hair back. All the while, Peyton continued to stare at her.

What was wrong? Had she made another workplace error?

Should she have kept her hair pulled back into the

tight elastic? Maybe so, but if she hadn't let the reddish-blond mass out of its tight confines, she wouldn't have gotten any relief from the unbearable throbbing above her right ear.

And the only way she could stay in the same room with Peyton and not completely lose her cool was to stop the throbbing.

When he finally spoke, he averted his gaze and said, "Now that you're back, do you think you can…um… handle things while I get my suitcase and grab a quick bite to eat?"

Suddenly, she found herself staring at his back. The man didn't even wait for her answer before he bolted out the front door.

Oh, no. She'd been right. He *had* come to the conclusion that she couldn't deal with things on her own. He was probably running out to call his boss right now and tell him the Brighton Valley store was such a mess that it wasn't worth saving.

She wanted to chase after him, but she couldn't leave the shop unattended.

But wait. He'd said that he was getting his suitcase. And he was coming back to stay in the apartment above the shop.

She needed to go upstairs and freshen things up. She had to change the bedding and get rid of the house-coat Cindy Carpenter kept up there for those days after her chemo treatments when Don wanted her close by so he could keep an eye on her while he worked. She also needed to make sure the kids had picked up any messes they might have made when they'd had their after-school snacks there yesterday.

"Tyler," she said, "help your sister with her spelling and watch the shop. I need to clean the apartment upstairs."

"You got it, Mom."

"And keep an eye out for Mr. Johnson. When he comes back, give me a heads-up."

"I'll give you two birdcalls to warn you," the boy said.

Megan blew out a sigh. "Just keep him in front and send Lisa to get me."

She couldn't afford to be anywhere but downstairs and hard at work when he returned.

Clay couldn't believe he'd run out of the store like a blushing teenager stumbling over his own tongue. He tried to tell himself that it was his low blood sugar, but he'd eaten enough of those amazing snickerdoodles to raise his glucose levels through the roof. Hopefully, it was just the lack of protein doing a real number on him.

It couldn't possibly be the way the beautiful single mom had pulled her hair free from its rubber band and had shaken out the silky locks right in front of him.

He hadn't seen hair that thick and luscious since… Well, since…he didn't know when. Megan Adams had such a natural beauty and such a wholesome way about her—just like the cheerleaders in high school he used to pine after, the ones who hadn't even known he'd existed.

In fact, Megan probably had been a cheerleader and one of the girls who wouldn't have given him the time of day back then. Probably still wouldn't, at least in his Peyton Johnson persona.

Hell, after looking at some of the invoices and computer records while she'd been out playing soccer mom, he had to wonder if she even knew the store existed.

The books were a disaster—from the bookkeeping to the mounds of overdue repairs. Clay definitely had his work cut out for him.

Clearly, Megan was in over her head and no amount of homemade cookies would make up for the fact that some immediate personnel changes would need to be made.

How was he going to turn the store around and not let on who he was?

Already he'd made the slip about Mia Hamm to Megan's daughter. Clay actually did know the World Cup–winning soccer player. He knew a lot of professional athletes and celebrities, thanks to all the charity events he supported and attended. And most of the athletes he associated with knew that they couldn't float through life on athleticism alone—unlike Todd Redding and some of the other guys on the high school football team. Not that Megan's daughter, with her matching braids and grass-stained knees, was anything like the jocks who used to pick on him back then.

Still, if he wasn't careful, he'd blow his cover before he got through the first day. He needed to get away from all that luscious red hair and those big brown eyes so he wouldn't get soft and say something that would give him away.

Taking a break and getting some solid food, like one of Caroline's juicy cheeseburgers, in his stomach would help.

Normally, he steered away from red meat and fried foods—ever since he'd moved to California, in fact. It had been part of his attempt to create a new identity to go along with the successful life he'd built for himself.

But he decided that he might as well enjoy a burger

and fries now, then get back to healthier choices once he figured out where he could find the nearest Whole Foods Market.

As he strode past the ice-cream store—damn, there were a lot of temptations in this town—his cell phone rang. He checked the caller ID, needing to make sure he answered with the right identity. After all, only his assistant knew Clay Jenkins and Peyton Johnson were the same man.

The display read Don Carpenter.

It was about time the store manager called him back. Where was he on a work day? And why in the world would he leave Clay's precious start-up business in the hands of that gorgeous but distracted and incompetent woman?

"This is Peyton Johnson," he answered.

"Don Carpenter here. I'm so sorry I missed your call earlier. I'm at the Brighton Valley Medical Center with my wife. They were running some tests when you rang."

Clay understood medical issues and emergencies came up, but why hadn't Don called to cancel their appointment? And why hadn't he hired a reputable backup employee?

"You and I were supposed to meet at noon today," Clay said.

"I could have sworn we scheduled that for Wednesday."

"Today *is* Wednesday."

"Oh, dear. Normally I take my Cindy in for her treatments on Tuesdays, which I did yesterday. But she passed out early this morning, and I had to bring her in to see her doctor today, and now they're running tests. So that's thrown me off-kilter. I'm sorry."

Cindy must be Don's wife, and the treatments he mentioned had to be pretty serious if they routinely took place at the hospital each week. Clay couldn't very well chastise the man for missing work because of his sick wife.

"Don't worry about it," Clay said. "I met with Megan. She showed me around and gave me access to everything I need to get started."

"Oh, good. Megan's a great gal. And she's been a big help at the store. The customers love her fresh-baked goods. Single mom, you know, with those two sweet kids."

Clay didn't know if *sweet* was the right word to describe Lisa and Tyler. In fact, one of those kids had been suspended today for not being sweet at all. Of course, Clay could forgive the kid his hacking attempts in an effort to even the score with a class bully. After all, he'd certainly been in Tyler's shoes back in the day. If Clay stuck around long enough, he'd have to...

Wait a second. What was he thinking?

"Megan's been a godsend," Don added. As he continued to sing her praises, Clay wondered if they were talking about the same woman.

"But you won't meet her when you come into town tomorrow," Don added. "Wednesday is her normal day off."

"*Today* is Wednesday," Clay repeated. "I'm in town *now*."

The conversation had just made a complete circle, and Clay was no more informed about the happenings at Zorba's than he'd been three hours ago.

"You're right," Don said. "I'm sorry. I didn't get much sleep last night. But I'm afraid I have to hang up now. The doctor is coming with Cindy's results. I'll see you at the shop tomorrow, Mr. Johnson."

Clay ended the call, then looked at the phone in his hand and blew out a sigh.

No wonder the shop was falling apart. Don was so caught up with his sick wife that he couldn't focus on the store. In fact, he'd had to hire in help—and incompetent help at that.

Did Clay even dare leave Megan alone long enough to grab a bite to eat?

Chapter Three

Clay opened the glass door to Caroline's Diner and scanned the interior of the small-town eatery, with its pale yellow walls and white café-style curtains on the front windows.

To the right of an old-fashioned cash register stood a refrigerated display case filled with desserts—each one clearly homemade. He studied the towering meringues and whipped-cream toppings on the pies, the four-layer chocolate cake, the deep-dish peach cobbler.

He glanced at a blackboard that advertised a full meal for only $7.99. In bright yellow chalk, Caroline had written, "What the Sheriff Ate," followed by, "Chicken-Fried Steak, Buttered Green Beans, Mashed Potatoes, Country Gravy and Cherry Cobbler."

The advertised special sounded delicious, but Clay had his heart set on a cheeseburger. Besides, he'd had a near run-in with Caroline's husband, Sheriff Jennings, once. And the old man had been sixty pounds overweight back then.

Clay doubted if the law enforcement officer could even buckle his gun belt after eating daily meals like that for the past seven years. Of course, Sam Jennings had to be retired by now.

Sally, a salt-and-pepper-haired waitress who'd worked at the diner back when Clay had been in high school—and probably much longer than that—stopped by his table and smiled. "Can I get you something to drink?"

"Water will be fine."

"Our iced tea is fresh brewed. How 'bout I get you a tall glass of that with your water?"

This was Texas. If he wanted to fit in, he should probably drink the nectar of his youth.

"Sure, but unsweetened, please."

Sally clucked her tongue in obvious disapproval, but Clay knew that if he wasn't careful, his belly would get just as large as old Sheriff Jennings's.

"You new in town, sugar, or just passing through?" Sally was a nice lady, but curious and a real talker.

While he was glad she hadn't recognized him, he wasn't eager to answer too many questions about himself. But then again, he'd gone over his made-up background several times on his flight and his drive into Brighton Valley, so he was prepared. And he hadn't had a chance to deliver it in full yet, especially since Megan kept running out of the store before they could really talk. So it wouldn't hurt to test it out on someone, especially when that someone was also likely to know all the town gossip.

Clay kept it brief, though, giving his fake name, mentioning that he was from the Geekon corporate offices and helping out at the computer store down the street.

"What a blessing you must be to Don Carpenter. He's had his hands full since poor Cindy's diagnosis. I sure hope she's feeling better now. That chemo can really take a lot out of a person. You know what I mean?"

No, Clay didn't know. He'd never had to deal with cancer. His own mother's bipolar disorder was the closest thing he'd come to dealing with someone's chronic illness.

But that certainly explained why Don was so concerned about his wife and why Megan had her kids at the shop this afternoon. If this was supposed to be her day off, Clay ought to cut her a little slack. But he still couldn't sit back and let the store go under.

"I met Megan Adams," he said. "It's nice that they have someone helping out at the store." Clay wasn't quite buying his comment, but he needed to fish for more information. And already the waitress who was dressed like Dolly Parton's mousy-haired sister was proving to be a useful tool.

"Don't you know it! I love that Megan to pieces. She's a wonderful mom and she's pure heaven in the kitchen. We sold out of her muffins this morning and only have a few more jars of her preserves left for the week. I know that girl needs the income from Zorba's, but just between you and me, she'd make a much better living selling her baked goods, jams and jellies than working part-time for Don Carpenter."

So Megan had a side job selling homemade goods to the diner? Well, he couldn't fault her for being industrious. And if her muffins were as good as her cookies, he could understand why they'd sold out.

But was she in dire financial straits? Would she be tempted to pilfer funds from the store?

Once he had some time alone with the books, that's what he intended to find out.

Two elderly women shuffled in and sat at one of the booths. Mindful not to take up too much of Sally's time, Clay put in his order for the double-bacon cheeseburger with an extra side of French fries.

He might end up gaining ten pounds, but clearly, patronizing Caroline's Diner was going to be one of the best ways for him to get information about his store—and the people running it.

Thirty minutes later, after he'd eaten his burger and finished every last fry on his plate, he let Sally talk him into taking a piece of peanut-butter pie to go.

It was still early and he planned to get his suitcase out of the SUV and into the upstairs apartment. Then he'd send Megan home so he could close up the shop and take a good look at the books. The pie would come in handy as a snack because he knew he'd be putting in some long hours tonight.

When he took his check up to the old-fashioned cash register, he glanced at the elderly women and saw them counting out the quarters from their coin purses. He pulled an extra twenty from his wallet. Then, using a pad and pen that rested on the counter, he scratched out a note to let Caroline know he intended to cover the ladies' meals, too.

After paying his own tab, he handed the surprised waitress a ten dollar bill as a tip and left the diner. On his way back to Zorba's, he set a slow pace, the memories bogging him down.

Maybe it was seeing the two women counting out their change and being reminded about how he'd once lived in a different world, how he'd once had to struggle to make ends meet, too. His mom might have brought home a paycheck, but he'd been the one to budget the money, pay the bills, buy the groceries and cook the meals. He'd also made sure she took her meds and got up each afternoon so she could go back to work at the lab and start the process all over again—that is, until she'd died.

Maybe seeing Megan with her son, acting like the protective and caring mom Clay had always wished for himself, had poked at some tender spot deep in his heart.

Either way, the past was playing havoc with him. But he did his best to shake it off and to put the memories behind him before returning to work.

As he reentered the shop, he spotted Lisa sitting at the front counter, doodling on what must have been her spelling homework.

"Hey, Mr. Johnson. Do you know anything about athletes who don't have to read? I heard that gymnasts get to go to school at home, but only for a couple of hours every day because they're too busy practicing at their gyms. Maybe I should switch from soccer to gymnastics."

The girl was asking Clay for advice? Heck, he didn't have any experience with children. He'd never had siblings. And he'd always avoided the kids who'd played sports in school. How was he supposed to know what she should play?

"Everyone needs to be able to read," he said. "Even gymnasts."

"What about softball? Mom signed me up for a sports camp this summer through the YMCA. I hope I get to try out all sorts of sports and can figure out which one will get me out of school the most."

"Why don't you like school?" Clay scanned the shop, looking around for Megan—or for anyone who could get him out of this awkward conversation.

And speaking of Megan, where was she?

He wanted to get started on the disaster of an office, and it should be nearly time to close up for the day.

"It's okay," Lisa said. "Our PE teacher, Mrs. Sanchez, is nice. And I like my friends and having recess. But I don't like doing seatwork. I'm not good at it. All the letters jumble around, and so I'd rather be outside."

No wonder the little girl felt more comfortable playing sports than doing her spelling. She was better at it. Clay had felt the same way when he'd been in school—only with sports instead of spelling. It had taken him years to figure out how to dribble a basketball, but once he got ahold of a computer and had his hands on a mouse and keyboard, his fingers had excelled for hours.

"Yes!" Tyler's voice shouted out from the back, calling Clay from his musing.

He couldn't allow himself to get soft. And where was Megan? Had she left again?

Clay headed to the back of the shop, where Tyler clicked furiously on a mouse at the workstation. He leaned over to look at the screen and saw the customer claim sticker on the computer's hard drive. Oh, no. The boy was messing with equipment that had been entrusted to Zorba's.

"Why are you on that computer?" Clay tried to keep the accusatory tone from his voice, but his frustration level was rising.

The ringing telephone interrupted him, and he headed toward the front of the store. Before he could reach the counter, Lisa picked up the receiver and said, "Zorba the Geek's Computer Repair Shop. Can I help you?"

This was way too much. A seven-year-old was answering the business phone, while a twelve-year-old was back here playing around with a customer's computer.

Where in the hell was their mother? Clay looked around the small space, his temper rising. Brighton Valley might be a small town, but that didn't account for the complete lack of professionalism he'd experienced since his arrival a few hours ago.

He had no idea how he'd keep himself from firing Megan on the spot when she returned.

"Tyler," Lisa's singsong voice called out from the opening between the two rooms. "Mr. Hochstein wants to know if you got that virus off his computer yet. He has an online poker tournament tomorrow night and needs it back by then."

"Yep." Tyler swiped at the keyboard and yelled back to his sister. "I just got the nasty little bugger. And I'm cleaning up the rest of his files right now. But he's got to stop going to those offshore betting websites, because that's how he got the virus in the first place. And he just got an instant message."

Lisa relayed the boy's response better than Clay had expected her to.

"Mr. Hochstein wants to know who's looking for him," the girl said.

"BigPokerMama213. There's a tournament tomorrow with a twenty-dollar buy-in."

As the girl repeated the message over the telephone, Clay wondered if they'd somehow broken some kind of law—besides the child labor law.

Did it matter that the kids weren't actually working or on the payroll? But what about participating in gambling?

He was also a little taken aback by Tyler's skill at fixing the computer, considering his age. He'd heard of the international betting virus that had a lot of software techs scrambling to immunize their systems from the havoc it could wreak. And this little boy—who'd just been suspended from the last two days of seventh grade—seemed to think that he'd single-handedly conquered the virus.

Clay would have to check it out, but if the boy had actually done that, technological interest and amazement took precedence over customer service.

"How'd you figure out how to fix that virus?" he asked.

As Tyler explained the process in depth, Clay realized the kid was onto something. But before he could respond, a creak sounded through the ceiling above. Apparently, Megan was upstairs in the apartment.

"I'd like to talk more about that," Clay said. "But go ahead and finish what you're doing."

Curious as to what Megan might be up to—or what she might be hiding—he left the kids in the shop and headed toward the stairway that led to the apartment.

Deciding to catch her in the act of ditching work or whatever she might be up to, he quietly slipped upstairs and entered the living room, which held a floral loveseat sofa, coffee table and small television set. Every-thing looked as if it had just been wiped down, and the rug bore fresh vacuum lines.

The small kitchen was tidy and the little table and chairs held a burning candle that smelled like vanilla.

Classic-rock music wafted from the bedroom, so Clay made his way in that direction. When he reached the doorway, he spotted Megan bent over the bed, tuck-ing the sheets into perfectly creased hospital corners. But the bedding wasn't anywhere near as intriguing as the view of Megan's lovely backside, her denim-clad hips swaying in tempo to the Fleetwood Mac song on the bedside clock radio.

Clay shoved his hands in his pockets, leaned against the doorjamb and continued to watch her mesmerizing movements, hoping Stevie Nicks never stopped singing.

Over the music, a boy's voice called out, "Whoops! Caw caaaaw. Caw caaaaw."

At the kid's lousy bird call, Megan froze, then slowly turned and caught Clay watching her from the doorway.

From the flush on her cheeks and the panic in her eyes, he figured that she'd just been belatedly warned of his approach.

By the way Peyton was gawking at her, Megan couldn't tell if he was annoyed at her for leaving her post at the store or if he was surprised to find her pre-paring the apartment for him. Either way, she straight-ened just as her children screeched into the bedroom doorway.

They gathered next to Peyton, with Tyler still mak-ing "caw caaaaw" sounds until Lisa gave him a little shove to quiet him.

It must have been blatantly obvious to the man that the kids had been trying to warn her of his presence, which embarrassed her all the more.

"What's going on?" Peyton asked.

"I was trying to freshen up the apartment. I had no idea you'd planned to stay here, and it wasn't ready."

"Is cleaning and scrubbing in your job description?" he asked.

Who'd he think he was? Her boss? She stiffened, then placed her hands on her hips. "I'm not going to apologize for being thoughtful or for showing a bit of small-town hospitality."

"I'm sorry. I didn't mean to sound unappreciative. It's just that…" He blew out a sigh, then raked a hand through his hair. "Well, let's just say that this day hasn't gone the way I'd expected it to."

Then that made two of them. Megan released a sigh of her own. "It's been a little out of the ordinary for me, too."

As the silence stretched between them, she took the opportunity to send the kids downstairs and to tell them to get their things together. Surely it had to be getting close to five o'clock.

As soon as she was alone with Peyton, she said, "Don meant to be here today, but that didn't work out. I came in to help him on my day off, but some childcare issues cropped up, which isn't the norm."

"I understand."

Did he? She hoped so. She also hoped that he didn't realize she'd been stretching the truth when she implied the kids weren't always here in the afternoons. She tried her best to keep them busy in after-school activities, but more often than not, especially with Tyler, one or both

of her children ended up spending time at the shop—
and in the apartment.

They stood like that for a moment, sizing each other
up in some kind of face-off.

With the bed behind her and his masculine frame
leaning against the doorjamb, arms crossed in a tense
yet sexy pose… Well, he wasn't exactly blocking her
escape route, but that was the problem. She didn't feel
like running off, and she really ought to. Because what
she found most troubling was the way her heart rate
was zipping along at an arousing pace, setting her hormones on high alert and sending her thoughts drifting
in a direction they had no business veering.

Peyton Johnson was a handsome man, and while
he was dressed casually, something about him flashed
City Boy in neon lights.

Still, she found him attractive. But being attracted
to a man wasn't the same thing as being interested in
him. And she definitely was not interested.

Besides, even if she *were* on the lookout for a
husband—or even a romantic interest—it certainly
wouldn't be a corporate yes-man who didn't even re-
side anywhere near the same town in which she lived.

After her divorce, she'd left Houston and put down
roots in Brighton Valley, where she'd finally been able
to give her kids the kind of home she'd always wanted
them to have—something she'd never been able to create for them while she'd been married to their father.

Breaking eye contact, she glanced at her watch. "It's
nearly five o'clock. Time for me to lock up the shop
and go home."

As she made her way to the bedroom doorway, Peyton stepped aside and let her pass. As he did so, she

caught a whiff of his cologne, something musky and exotic that sent her blood racing, her hormones reeling and her heart thumping.

She had no idea what brand of aftershave he used— or what stores would carry something so…

Well, she had no way of knowing if it was costly, but she'd pay a pretty penny to buy it as a gift for her man—if she had a man and the pennies to spare. She'd never smelled the like.

Maybe it wasn't just the scent alone. Maybe it was the way it blended with the pheromones he gave off. She didn't know for sure.

But as intoxicating and alluring as she'd found it to be, that only made her want to steer clear of the man the best that she could.

Because she'd come to distrust her choices when it came to men and sexual attraction. And something told her that Peyton Johnson, like his scent, would linger with a woman long after he left town—a life-changing, heartbreaking memory a woman wasn't likely to forget.

Chapter Four

The following morning, after dropping Lisa off at school, Megan pulled into her regular parking space in the alley behind the shop.

She needed to deliver this morning's fresh batch of peach-crumble muffins to Caroline at the diner before starting work. So she took the linen-covered basket out of her backseat and grabbed the oversize breakfast burrito she'd wrapped in foil. Then she locked the car.

As she made her way toward the back entrance of the diner, she risked an upward glance at the apartment over Zorba's. The shutters were closed. Peyton was most likely still asleep, which meant he'd probably been up late last night snooping through all their files.

She'd stayed up most of the night, too, but her time had been spent in the kitchen, baking and preparing more jams and preserves for the farmers' market held in town square on the third Sunday of each month. She'd hoped her work would be a diversion for her worries, but she hadn't been able to keep her thoughts from straying to the sexy and suspicious stranger who'd kept her second-guessing everything he did or said.

Did he have another agenda besides helping them get the new accounting system up and running?

Could he be trusted to do only that particular job and not run back to corporate with reports of how bad things actually were at the Brighton Valley store?

She lifted the basket containing the fruits of her labor, rested it on one hip and strode into the diner through the open back door.

Caroline, who'd been a friend of Megan's late grandmother, sat at the butcher-block counter, making notes and ordering supplies. Annie, the cook, was busy frying eggs and flipping pancakes, while Sally hollered out breakfast orders through the open window between the front of the restaurant and the kitchen.

After Megan had divorced Todd and moved home to live with her mom, Caroline had suggested that Megan sell some of the extra peaches and plums that grew in the family orchard at the farmers' market. Since she'd been left in dire financial straits thanks to Todd's wild and reckless spending habits, she'd jumped on the idea of earning some extra money.

To liven up the boring displays of fruit, she'd set out a few jars of the jellies and preserves she'd canned, along with a few muffins.

As a child and the only girl in the family, she'd spent the summers on Gram's farm, where she'd learned to cook and bake, memorizing all her grandmother's recipes, especially the preserves, which had won Gram many a blue ribbon at the county fair each year. Still, she'd been surprised when her preserves had sold out well before the peaches and plums had.

Caroline had been shopping for produce for her restaurant that day and had told Megan that some people didn't have the patience or skill to make things from scratch anymore. They'd rather buy the ready-made product than mess up their own kitchens. Then Caroline had purchased the rest of the peaches left on the table and handed them back to Megan, commissioning her to make some more muffins and preserves and asking her to bring them into the diner on Monday morning.

Although Caroline shared Megan's love for cooking, her husband was now retired and she'd been trying to cut back on her own hours at the diner, as well. So having some of the bakery items Megan made would allow the older woman to spend more time in the mornings with her husband, Sam.

Megan's wallet had certainly benefited from the arrangement. But it hadn't been enough, especially since she'd wanted to get a tutor for Lisa, something her parents hadn't been able to afford for her. And since Todd had left the state nearly three years ago after making only a couple of child-support payments, life had still been a bit of a struggle. But then, hadn't it always been?

That was why she'd taken the job at Zorba's. It had allowed her to supplement her income and provide health insurance for her and her kids.

"I hope you brought in more of the peach-jalapeño jam," Caroline told her when she set the basket down on the counter. "We have the Rotary meeting here tomorrow. And Mayor Mendez always eats about ten of my biscuits and at least a jar of that jam all by himself."

"I only have one jar left, so if he runs out, he'll have to pour some of your famous sausage gravy over his biscuits. I was going to make a double batch yesterday, but Don called me in at the last minute to cover for him while he took Cindy to the doctor. And from there, my whole day went downhill."

Megan went on to fill in her friend about Tyler's suspension and the arrival of Peyton Johnson from the Geekon headquarters.

"Yep, I heard all about him," Caroline said.

"Already?"

Caroline used her thumb to point toward Sally.

Megan shouldn't have been surprised. Sally was a sweetheart, but she also talked up a storm and knew everything there was to know about Brighton Valley, its residents and its visitors.

"Sally said he stopped in for an early dinner. He was real sweet, although a bit on the shy side, and ate like he hadn't had a good home-cooked meal in ages. Then he paid for the Franco sisters' dinner and left a very generous tip."

"Did Sally mention that the guy could also get Don and me in trouble with the corporate office, which would ruin all our lives?" Megan knew she was being a bit dramatic, but just because Peyton was a hungry man who'd paid for two elderly women's dinners, didn't mean he wasn't also a snooping corporate suit trying to find out what she'd kept under wraps for the past few months.

"Nope. But she did mention that he was extremely good-looking. 'Handsome as sin,' I believe was the phrase she used. And she hasn't called a man that since that Burt Reynolds look-alike passed through town last summer."

Megan wasn't ready to concede to any of Peyton Johnson's good qualities just yet. Even the physical ones. But she did have to admit that they'd been evident right from the start—not that she'd allow herself to be swayed by them.

She doubted Peyton knew what small-town life was even like. Sure, he might have been nice to a hardworking and friendly waitress. And so what if he'd picked up the dinner tab for two elderly sisters who were living on a very limited income?

The fact remained that his loafers were brand-spanking new. He was obviously a city boy born and bred, and she couldn't wait for him to go right back to wherever he'd come from.

"I'll try to get you some more preserves by Monday," she said as she headed to the door. She had to get to Zorba's before Don arrived so she could help finesse the meeting between the two men and help smooth things over if necessary.

She already had the breakfast burrito to take to Don, but right before she stepped out the back door of the diner, she turned and went back to the basket to grab a muffin for Peyton.

After the mess he'd walked into yesterday, she might need to sweeten up the quiet but calculated corporate big shot.

Clay had barely lifted his head off the pillow when a car door slammed outside in the alley below.

He reached for the nightstand and felt around for his trademark black-framed glasses before remembering that he'd brought only contact lenses with him. So he squinted at the bedside clock. Eight-thirty? Already?

Man, he could use a double shot of caffeine after the late night he'd had. He sat up and ran a hand through his hair, still not used to the shorter length.

Today was going to be even more grueling than yesterday, especially if he had to deal with any disgruntled customers, as well as inept employees—and maybe even a child or two.

So far the only promising things the Brighton Valley shop had to offer the corporate office, which they wouldn't appreciate, were Tyler's debugging skills and Megan's cookies and homey touches in the apartment.

Megan.

In spite of his negative first impression of her as an employee, he hadn't been able to stop thinking of her in the bedroom, blushing like a coed while she'd hustled her kids home.

After she'd gone downstairs and left the store, he'd continued to stand in the middle of the small apartment, listening to the radio station play classic-rock music until the commercial break. And even then, it had been several minutes before his brain had been able to shift gears so that he could function well enough to get some work done.

Why had the woman thrown him so off course?

He never got tongue-tied around the fairer sex. Well, that wasn't exactly true. But he certainly hadn't been at a loss for words around them in the past seven years. Not since he'd single-handedly invented what the media had termed "a computer for the generations" and established a multibillion-dollar industry with his GeekMart and Zorba chains.

Still, he hadn't been this uncomfortable around a woman since he'd been in high school.

Maybe that was what it was about Megan. She reminded him of the pretty girls who'd only dated football players and had never given a guy like him the time of day.

Was that why he'd found himself attracted to her? And why he hadn't been able to get any work done until after dark, when he'd had to finally force himself to push the thoughts of the sexy single mom out of his mind?

Last night, he'd just started to make a little headway when around midnight he'd stumbled across a magazine in a drawer in Don Carpenter's desk that could have been his undoing.

At the time, he'd been looking for at least ten invoices that should have been accompanying just as many computers that had been tagged for repairs. But when he'd pulled open the old wooden drawer, he'd spotted a familiar picture—or parts of it, anyway. He'd had to move a battered floppy-disk drive and a moldy doughnut off the cover of the magazine to see the entire image, but he'd definitely recognized his own shoulder-length hair and black-framed glasses.

He shouldn't have been surprised to see the image of a successful man staring back at him, but being stuck in Brighton Valley made him feel like an eighteen-year-old again. And seeing himself on the magazine cover had served to remind him of how far he'd come.

Once he'd realized what he'd spotted, he'd thrown out the doughnut and pulled the year-old issue of *Software Weekly* from the drawer. The last thing he needed was for someone to see the photo and read the interview he'd grudgingly agreed to. He might be clean-shaven and wearing contact lenses now, but it wouldn't take a brain surgeon to realize that Clay Jenkins and Peyton Johnson were one and the same.

Of course, he doubted anyone around Zorba's would figure it out even if he pinned the magazine to the bulletin board by the restroom.

Not that Megan wasn't sharp enough to spot any similarities. She probably could if she stayed in the same room with him for longer than two minutes at a time.

And then there was the store's manager. Clay didn't even know *what* to think of Don Carpenter. But the man's mind was clearly not on business these days.

Last night, when he'd gone over to the office shredder to put the magazine through it, Clay had found the missing invoices piled up in the "to be shredded" box. And the books and accounts were in complete disarray.

Megan had been right, though. There was no way they could convert the accounting to a new computerized program until they organized the current old-fashioned system. And that was going to take much longer than Clay had anticipated.

A second car door slammed shut outside, and Clay suspected that both employees had finally arrived. He hoped so, because it was going to take all three of them to sort through the mess he'd uncovered last night.

Either way, it was time to get to work. So he climbed out of bed. After a quick shower, he made his way downstairs, where he caught the aroma of fresh-perked coffee. It wasn't Starbucks, but he'd take what he could get in this Podunk town.

When he stepped into the back office, he spotted Megan standing at a tiny counter, taking mugs from the small overhead cupboard. She was wearing a pair of black slacks today and a green blouse. Her long red hair had been pulled back into a ponytail again, as if she knew she'd be bent over a desk all day.

It was good that she'd planned to work, although he'd always been partial to long hair that flowed around a woman's shoulders—much as hers had yesterday when she'd removed the rubber band.

Don Carpenter, a sixty-something man with a receding gray hairline, sat behind the biggest desk. He wore a short-sleeved polyester polo shirt, the light blue fabric stretched tightly across his well-rounded belly. He looked up when Clay entered and scrunched his weathered brow.

"Mr. Carpenter," Megan said, as she hurried from the coffeepot to his desk and placed a gentle hand on his shoulder. "This is Peyton Johnson. He's the accountant from Geekon who came to help us convert our books to the new computerized accounting system. He's staying in the apartment upstairs while he's here."

"Right, right," Don said. "I'm afraid you caught us at a bad time. We've gotten a little behind, although I hope to get caught up soon. Maybe it would be best if you could come back next month."

"I'm afraid that's not possible," Clay said.

"Here, Don." Megan pushed a foil-wrapped package at her boss, doing that forced-smile thing again. "This is the breakfast burrito you wanted."

Was she purposely trying to interrupt their conversation?

"No thanks, dear. I already had breakfast this morning."

Her smile faded, and after a beat, she turned to

Clay—apparently in default. "Would you like an egg-and-cheese burrito, Mr. Johnson? I also have a peach muffin."

Whether he'd been second choice or not didn't matter. Breakfast sounded pretty darn good. And it smelled good, too. "Sure, thanks."

Don Carpenter settled back into his desk chair and returned to reading whatever paperwork he'd been looking at moments ago, then he slipped on a pair of headphones as if a corporate accountant had never even entered the store.

Clay could have made an issue, he supposed, but his stomach rumbled at the sight of that muffin and the foil-wrapped breakfast. If nobody else was in any sort of hurry to get to work, he might as well take a bite.

"So, Megan," he said, as he unwrapped the burrito, "what's your job here? Besides being the resident chef."

"Oh, I'm not a chef. That's just what I made the kids for breakfast. And I always bring in something for... Well, when I have extras, I bring them in. Anyway, I work here part-time. I've been doing some bookkeeping and customer service and basically helping out wherever I can."

"No kids with you today?" Clay looked behind her toward the front of the store.

She crossed her arms, the movement causing the fabric of her green blouse to tug and pop a button out of the hole, revealing a glimpse of her yellow bra.

Apparently she didn't realize what she was flashing, and he didn't think he ought to be the one to point it out. So he looked back to Don, who continued to shuffle through the papers on his desk, studying each one carefully.

Clay had already gone through those same papers last night and knew for a fact that they were all outdated memos, not a single one relevant. He turned back to Megan.

When she caught him looking at her, she quickly smiled again.

Yep, she was covering for her boss, all right. But covering *what* exactly? The fact that he'd been neglecting his work? Or was there more to it than that?

"Coffee?" she asked.

He must have looked as if he needed it, because she proceeded to pour two cups, even though he had his mouth full and hadn't been able to answer.

"Cream and sugar?" she asked.

He nodded, and she added two packets of sugar. Then she scooped out two spoonfuls of nondairy creamer and mixed it in, too. After giving it a little stir, she handed the cup to him.

The other coffee she left black, keeping it for herself. He was surprised someone who cooked so many treats didn't seem to enjoy sweet things herself.

"How's the burrito?" she asked. "Is it still warm?"

"Uh, yeah. It's perfect." And it really was. Clay took another bite and followed it up with a sip of coffee.

No one had ever taken an interest in what he ate or how it tasted. He'd grown up cooking for himself and his mom, who'd rarely cared if the grilled cheese sandwich he'd made them was burned or if the frozen chicken pot pie wasn't cooked all the way through.

But here was Megan, a complete stranger, looking at him as though her single mission in life was to make sure that everything he put in his mouth was just right.

When she raised her own cup to her lips, he chanced

a second peek at her green blouse, which had popped another button, allowing him to catch a better glimpse of that yellow lace bra and even a flash of skin.

Get a grip. He was no longer a teenager on hormone overload. Besides, she was an *employee.* And as if that weren't enough, she also had kids, and Clay never dated women with children.

That was it! He needed to talk about mom things with her.

"So, uh, how's the little hacker this morning? Is his split lip healing?"

His question wiped the smile, one that had been a little more genuine than forced, right off her face.

Shouldn't he have brought that up? He had no idea what else to talk to her about, so asking her about her kids seemed like neutral territory.

She gave a little shrug, which caused the fabric of her blouse to tug at the unbuttoned gap. "Tyler? He's at home with a very, very long list of chores to finish before I check on him at noon."

"You didn't have to leave him at home." Clay looked at the waiting repairs that Don didn't seem in any hurry to get to. "We could've found some things for him to do around here."

Actually, Clay was pretty sure his legal department wouldn't be okay with having a twelve-year-old in the shop working on repairs. But they were so backed up, and the kid could certainly do some of the easier things.

"Are you kidding?" Megan laughed—a real one, complete with a genuine, bright-eyed smile, the sight and sound of which warmed Clay in a way the coffee never could. "Working in here with the computers would have been a reward for Tyler, not a punishment."

The teenage geek inside Clay felt a tug of sympathy for the boy. And the grown man felt a tug of something entirely different for the boy's pretty mother.

"Speaking of work," Clay said, trying to shake both unwelcome feelings and renew his focus. "Should we get started?"

Megan's real smile faded, but she managed to paste the fake one back in place. "Of course. Where do you want to begin?"

"Why don't we get the new accounting program loaded up and running so we can start entering last year's fiscal reports? Once we have that established, we can input this year's billings and receivables onto the spreadsheet. That way we can see where we stand."

"Sounds good."

As Clay carried his coffee cup, which was now almost empty, toward Don's desk and the main office computer, Megan whirled her petite frame in front of him and pointed to an empty desk that he could have sworn wasn't there last night. "Where did that come from?"

"I set it up for you this morning." She force-smiled again and Clay couldn't help wondering if many people fell for that overdone grin. But he wasn't going to comment on it. Yet.

He looked at the freshly wiped-down work surface that must have been buried under a pile of unfiled paperwork last night. Now the desk held only a jar of recently sharpened pencils, a blank notepad and a fresh daisy in a small ceramic vase.

"I'll need the master computer to upload the program." He looked back at Mr. Carpenter's desk. "Isn't that it?"

"Um, it used to be. But I figured we should just start a new program with a fresh computer." She gestured toward a wall of refurbished PCs for sale. "We can make use of one of these."

Her fake smile, some home-baked goods, a clean apartment and a spiffy new desk complete with a flower must be part of some smoke-and-mirrors routine to keep him from seeing the big picture.

"But won't Don need access to the master computer on his desk?" Clay asked.

"I'm sure he'd rather have it over here where it won't get in his way. He's been a little, uh, overwhelmed lately with his wife being sick and all. He's really busy with other stuff, so why don't you and I take care of it and not bother him with the little details."

But that's the guy's job, Clay wanted to yell loud enough for the manager to hear despite the headphones.

Don Carpenter was being *paid* to be bothered with the little details. Yet before Clay could argue, Megan placed the muffin on his new desk and began to pull down one of the old PCs from the shelf. She might know her way around a mixing bowl, but clearly she knew nothing about computers. The new Geekon500 sitting in the box on the lower shelf would be best suited for the master computer.

He stopped her. "While you file away some of those documents over there, I'll set up the computer."

She hesitated, then moved to the back of the room, picking up loose papers and putting them into stacks.

As Clay bit into the tempting peach muffin she'd left on his desk, he had to agree with something Sally the waitress had told him yesterday. Megan *was* heaven in the kitchen. And after seeing her moving around his bedroom yesterday, he thought she looked as if she could be heaven in there, as well.

There he went again. What was he thinking? He had a strict no-dating-in-the-workplace policy. And he wasn't about to break his own rule now, despite the fact that last night he'd ended up downloading the entire Fleetwood Mac *Greatest Hits* album onto his personal laptop as he sorted through the office, thinking about the sway of Megan's hips while listening to the music.

She wasn't his type of woman. And even if computer geeks like him, rather than star athletes, actually were her type of man, it wouldn't be fair to get too close to her. After all, he still might need to fire her, although not for embezzlement, as he'd originally thought he might have to—or for incompetence, which he'd now begun to doubt.

GeekMart and Zorba the Geek hired only corporate-minded employees, which the gorgeous mom clearly was not.

Trouble was, something about Megan had gotten under Clay's skin, something that had him thinking about small-town life, about holding hands at the movies on a Friday night and stopping by the local ice-cream shop afterward for a banana split.

And Clay's new life had blasted light-years away from a world like that. In fact, he was eager to zip out of here and back to the city as quickly as he could.

But something told him he'd have to give Megan Adams one hell of a severance package so he could once again leave town without a backward glance.

Chapter Five

Megan had no idea how many times she'd looked up from the stack of papers on her desk. It wasn't even lunchtime, but her frustration level was growing by the minute.

The prices and totals she could handle just fine, but as usual, the letters swam before her eyes and jumped around the page until that old familiar ache knotted at her temples.

You can do it, Meggie. Just concentrate.

Her mom's advice might have worked back when she was in elementary school, but how was she supposed to concentrate with the sexy corporate accountant sitting just a few feet away from her?

She refused to glance over at Peyton again and instead tried to focus on the invoice in front of her.

Just because reading doesn't come easily for you

doesn't mean you're not a smart girl. Look at how well you can do other things.

It never seemed to matter how many times her mom reminded her how quickly she could add a column of numbers or how often Gram had praised her ability to memorize recipes and quickly convert cups to pints and quarts; Megan had always felt like a confused first grader when it came to reading. And while she'd finally learned to compensate for the disability by the time she'd graduated from high school, she still struggled with the notations on the invoices, especially when written in Don's illegible scrawl.

To make matters worse, she couldn't find the missing paperwork that Don had managed to leave in various places all over the shop—or figure out his weird filing system, even though he'd tried to explain it to her. But once she did, she'd be able to sort everything in a way that made sense to her.

She knew a computerized accounting system—especially in a store that repaired and sold computers!—was the ideal solution. But that would require her to learn an entirely new way of doing things, which might not be easy. However, if someone with a little patience took the time to go over the instructions, she knew she would catch on.

Trouble was, Peyton Johnson was here to do just that, but he was the last person in the world she wanted to sit next to her and point out anything, especially the intricacies of the digital age.

Maybe if he taught the new program to Tyler, then her son could show her. But presenting that idea to the corporate accountant was sure to go over like sprigs of poison oak in a pair of long johns, which meant she was back to square one.

So she took another shot at deciphering Don's notation on the invoice she'd been reading. The machine in question was a laptop, but she had no idea who'd even brought it in, let alone what brand it was or the reason it needed to be repaired. And she hated to ask Don to look the paper over while Peyton was here because she hated to point out yet one more reason they were so behind the times.

In her frustration, she risked another glance at the man seated across from her.

Peyton had almost perfect posture as he typed diligently away on the keyboard in front of him. He'd rolled up his shirt sleeves to his elbows, revealing a smattering of hair on his well-muscled forearms.

She studied his strong tan fingers moving across the plastic letters and numbers, wondering if she was more envious of his ability to quickly and effortlessly type out the words or if she was merely jealous of the keyboard's luck in being the recipient of such smooth and solid strokes.

As his right hand reached for the mouse, she shifted in her desk chair and imagined him reaching for her....

Oh, for Pete's sake. What was wrong with her? She might have been without a man for longer than she cared to ponder, but she wasn't interested in doing anything to change that. At least, not unless she found someone who was more interested in sharing an emotional relationship before a physical one—no matter how hot and heavy it promised to be.

She had two kids, a shattered happily-ever-after

dream and a barely recovering FICO score to remind her that all sex and swagger made for bad husbands.

Too bad she hadn't listened more closely to Gram, who'd warned her to stay away from the boys who raced to scoop up the overly ripe fruit off the ground rather than wait for the perfect peach to ripen before climbing up into the tree to pick it at just the right time.

However, if she kept sitting here staring at Peyton and letting the tingle in her feminine core continue, she'd be in danger of letting her ripe peach fall directly into his lap.

"You know," Megan said, pushing her chair away from her desk, "I'm going to run to Caroline's and pick up some lunch. Anyone want me to bring something back?"

Don, who was still wearing his headphones while fixing one of the computers that had been brought in for repair, appeared to be oblivious to her announcement, which had rung out a little louder than she'd planned. But Peyton studied her in awe.

Or had her voice and sudden movement merely startled the man?

"Sure. You can pick up something for me." Peyton reached into his wallet, pulled out a twenty and handed it to her.

"What would you like?" she asked.

"Surprise me." His trust, at least when it came to his meal order, took her aback. And she found it difficult to break away from his gaze, which seemed to wrap around her, tethering her in place.

Finally noticing the activity around him, Don took off his headphones. "What's going on?"

"Lunchtime," Megan said. "Want me to pick up something at the diner for you?"

"Actually, I'm starving. But I promised Cindy I'd go home and make her some lunch. I think I'll whip up my cheesy broccoli soup. She hasn't been able to keep much down after her chemo rounds, and that ought to sit well. But go ahead and pick up something for Mr. Johnson. The two of you can eat while you mind the shop for me."

Knowing about Cindy's lactose intolerance, Megan doubted Don's wife would want his soup, but her boss was out the door before she could comment about the sick woman's dietary issues.

It was just as well, though. Don was so distracted that having him away from the office would be one less stress for her to worry about today.

Megan turned back to Peyton and pasted on her best cheerleader smile, feeling a bit too much like a beauty-pageant contestant professing her wish for world peace. She'd have to watch that, though. She'd been trying so hard to put on a happy face ever since his arrival that she feared her jaws would lock.

His presence had also brought on a chronically spiked heart rate, especially when he looked at her, as he was now....

What was he looking at? Not her eyes.

She followed his gaze down to her chest, where her blouse had come unbuttoned and now gaped open.

Oh, for goodness' sake. She turned her back, quickly righting her wardrobe malfunction and putting herself back together.

She crossed her arms before facing him, making sure the buttons hadn't popped open again. As she turned, she snuck a glance at him and caught him grinning. She frowned, and he averted his gaze to the keyboard.

Good. Now they were both uneasy. And he surely was because each time she'd stolen a peek at him earlier, he'd been typing away without the need to look at the keys. And now he was concentrating on each letter as though every little tap of his fingers were a life-or-death matter.

And maybe it was, for she feared Peyton Johnson would be the death of her—or at least of the Brighton Valley store. Earlier this morning, she'd come across a report Don had meant to send into the corporate office and, apparently, had neglected to. She wasn't an accountant, but it was clear to her that the store was struggling to stay afloat—something Peyton would figure out on his own, if he hadn't done so already.

She felt as though she was sitting on some kind of powder keg. How was she ever going to get through the next few hours, let alone the next couple of days, without all heck breaking loose?

As Peyton typed, she grabbed her purse and took her leave, glad to put some space between them, if only for a few minutes. The break would also provide her some time to check on Tyler. She couldn't very well drive out to the farm, especially with Don gone, and she didn't want to call him while Peyton could hear her doing so.

But first she'd get her breathing a little more under control. Maybe she ought to walk around the block several times and cool down before she headed into the diner.

Sally was a smart woman and the last thing Megan needed was for the well-meaning waitress to think that there was a potential romance brewing. There was no telling what Sally would do or say if she thought Megan was getting all sorts of flustered over some hunky visitor from the city.

And if truth be told, she *was* getting flustered. The man was too darn handsome for his own good. And if they were forced to work alone together the rest of the afternoon, and the button on her blouse popped open again, ripe peaches could start falling all over the shop.

After a brisk walk, during which she'd called home, Megan slipped her cell phone into her pants pocket. It had been a long time since she'd found herself attracted to a man, and she wasn't quite sure what to do with it— especially since Peyton Johnson was the last man in the world she needed to find attractive.

He wasn't from Brighton Valley, which was where she'd set down permanent roots. And he would be moving on soon, which she really ought to be thankful for since he could cause both her and Don to lose their jobs.

Trouble was, on top of the problems at work, she had enough to juggle these days, what with keeping up the family homestead for her mom and stepdad while they were traveling and running her side business venture of making and selling jams and preserves.

Then there were the ongoing single-mom worries of trying to raise a daughter with learning disabilities and a son who was not only being bullied at school but who'd reached adolescence and was no longer as happy and as forthcoming as he'd once been.

But now that she'd gotten outdoors and away from the hunky accountant, she was thinking a bit more clearly and feeling more in control.

The phone call to Tyler had certainly helped. He'd

assured her that he'd picked at least two crates of plums from the tree—and that he hadn't fallen off the ladder while doing so. He'd also promised her that he'd stayed off the computer and that he'd completed his long list of chores. He should be okay by himself until she got home after picking up Lisa from school.

So now all she had to do was finish her shift at the store, which required working with Peyton for another couple of hours.

She just hoped that bringing in lunch would be enough of a distraction to get them through the next hour or two before Don returned to the shop, which meant she had to be alone with the hunky corporate accountant for only another two hours—tops.

"I'll take two tuna salads and two unsweetened iced teas, to go," she told Sally.

"Oh, honey. Don doesn't ever order our tuna salad. Says we don't use enough mayo." Sally had a pencil tucked behind her ear, but she never seemed to need it when writing down an order for the locals. She'd been working for Caroline for so long that she knew everyone's preferences by heart. "I swear that man could be a poster child for the risks of high cholesterol. He has the worst diet. And with poor Cindy going through all that chemo business, Don's little heart must be working overtime with all the stress and what not. Maybe you should just get him the grilled chicken breast."

"Oh, it's not for Don. He went home to make Cindy's lunch."

"Not the cheesy broccoli soup again, I hope?"

"I'm afraid so."

Sally tsked. "I've told Don a hundred times that he'd do better to open up a bag of chips and try to pass off that greasy stuff as dip at his Rice University tailgating party. Poor Cindy's sensitive tummy can't handle something that heavy and spicy. I'll have Armando run her over a cup of the chicken-and-rice soup we made fresh today."

Megan looked at the busboy Sally was nodding at and was reminded of why she loved small-town life. All the neighbors looked after each other. They might know everyone's business and gossip from time to time, but they pulled together to take care of their own.

"So who's the other tuna salad for? That eye candy those bigwigs at Zorba's sent over to help y'all out?"

"You mean Mr. Johnson?" If Megan were going to concede that Peyton was any type of candy—for the eyes or otherwise—he'd be those deceptive little chocolate truffles. They might look pretty and chocolaty on the outside, but when you bit into them, gooey cherry cordial gel shot out all over the place.

No, those kinds of candies, sweet and yummy as they might look, could make a real mess of things.

"Of course I mean Mr. Johnson," Sally said. "You don't have any other handsome hunks working over there, do you?"

"No, it's just that I see him in a more professional light since I'm his coworker." Maybe if Megan could convince Sally that she hadn't noticed Peyton's physical attributes, she could convince herself, as well.

"Oh, honey, you got to open your horizons a bit more. You've been divorced a long time, and there ain't nothin' wrong with sampling a taste of the different types of sugar out there."

Uh-oh. Was that another candy reference? Megan wanted to tell Sally that she didn't have the time or the inclination to end up with a cavity, thank you very much, but luckily, Mayor Mendez came in.

He greeted Megan. "I was just going to stop by the shop on my way back to city hall after lunch. I dropped off my wife's computer last week, and I was wondering if it was repaired yet."

Probably not. And if he came in, she'd offer him a cookie to appease him. But that probably wouldn't work nearly as well as the sale that was going on, the one Peyton had told Riley about.

"I'll check on your wife's computer as soon as I return to the shop," Megan said. "But if it's not ready, Zorba's is running an awesome special. Peyton Johnson, one of the corporate reps, is there now, and he can tell you all about it. Apparently you can get a new Geekon Blast for a hundred dollars."

"No kidding? That's hard to believe."

"I felt the same way, but I spoke to a woman named Zoe at the Houston office, and she verified that price. I'm not sure how long the sale will last, but it certainly can't be very long."

"You've got that right," Caroline said. "A hundred dollars for a brand-new laptop, especially a Geekon, is a steal. I'm going to have to buy a couple for the office and one for home. And I'll make sure to get them today."

At that, Sally piped in. "I've been meaning to buy myself a computer, too. I've been learning how to email on an old one my friend loaned me last year. I'll stop by the shop as soon as I get off work."

Maybe if word spread in town and the store sold enough computers at the sale price, the corporate office would see them in a better light. Megan certainly hoped so. These days, Don needed all the luck and good press help he could get.

"How is Catherine feeling?" Sally asked the mayor. "That morning sickness can really be a drag."

The mayor's wife had been a city girl who'd fallen in love with him and settled in Brighton Valley. She'd given up the bright lights for small-town life, although with a husband like Ray Mendez, Megan could hardly blame her. Just about every single woman in town had set her sights on the tall, dark and handsome rancher/politician until Catherine Loza won his heart. And now his wife ran a dance school in Wexler and was expecting their second child.

"Oh, goodness," Sally said. "Here I am, dawdling and spending my tip money on a new computer and forgetting to place your order for those tuna salads."

Actually, Megan didn't mind the excuse to stay away from the shop for a while. Or to have the opportunity to promote those much-needed sales of the Geekon Blast.

"I know you're probably eager to get back to the store," Sally said, "but a young stud like Peyton Johnson needs something heartier than some boring old greens and a scoop of our famous tuna. Why don't I fix him up with the tamale pie that's on special today? That boy sure has an appetite. He put away a juicy burger and a large order of fries yesterday."

Sally was probably right, although Megan wasn't sure how he kept his body in such good shape if he didn't follow a healthy diet.

And what a shape his body was in. His athletic legs filled out his slacks to perfection and his arms looked as if they could lift her into any position he wanted her in.

There she went again. She had to stop thinking about

him that way. Maybe the tamale pie was a good idea. If he put on some weight, she might not find him nearly as attractive.

"Good idea," Megan told Sally. "You better make that a sweetened iced tea with a side order of fries. Oh, and a piece of the three-layer chocolate cake."

But the extra calories she was adding to his lunch wouldn't do anything about her short-term problem.

How was she going to keep her distance from him for the next couple of hours? She needed to make him less appealing *now*.

As Sally turned to place the order with the cook, Megan called out, "And extra onions on that tamale pie, as well as jalapeño peppers."

Maybe if she didn't catch a whiff of his peppermint-fresh breath, she wouldn't be inclined to daydream about getting up close and personal with the guy—or seeing if his kisses tasted as good as she thought they might.

Clay had the master computer up and running, but the internet connection was so sketchy he had to call the cable company and ask for a service tech to come by the store. As a result, he hadn't made anywhere near as much headway this morning as he'd intended. But that didn't mean he wasn't ready to find something else to focus on in the afternoon.

By the time Megan returned to the store with lunch, he was ready for a break and that new focus. And damned if she didn't give him one when she entered the shop, set down the box with the takeout order from Caroline's Diner and faced him with that button on her blouse having busted loose once again.

Should he tell her? Or should he just enjoy the sight of yellow lace and the hint of bare skin?

He didn't think the blouse she'd chosen to wear was too small. The problem seemed to be that her breasts were a bit too...

Well, hell, there was no way he could possibly classify them as too large. They were actually just right. Perfect.

Must be the buttonholes. Or the soft silky material that looked just slippery enough to...

Oh, for cripes' sake. He had no idea what had caused the problem, but he certainly wouldn't complain. And she had nice taste in undergarments, too. Wholesome yet sexy.

"The special was the hot tamale pie," Megan said.

Hot tamale, huh? Yet he wasn't talking about the plate of food she was unwrapping.

"Are you hungry?" she asked.

Seriously? He was growing hungrier by the minute. But as she placed the meal in front of him, he said, "Looks good. I've had a real craving for something hot and spicy."

"If you like hot and spicy as well as sweet," she said, "then I might have just the thing for you."

He just bet she did. And something told him they didn't come any sweeter or hotter than Megan Adams. But if she was suggesting more than lunch, if she thought that she could tempt him to turn his back on all the problems facing the Brighton Valley store, then he had even more reason to fire her.

"I make a spicy chili preserve that Caroline can't keep on the shelf," Megan said. "I'll have to bring some in for you to try tomorrow morning, along with one of my homemade biscuits."

She was talking about *jam?*

He stole a glance at her, watched her placing the food out on their desks.

So she wasn't coming on to him? That was a relief.

And yet a bit disappointing at the same time. And why was that? Sure, she had pretty hair and an alluring scent. But she was older than he was—she had to be unless she'd had her son when she was ten. She was also a single mother. So why did he find her so darn appealing?

She wasn't at all like the sophisticated and stylish women he normally dated. She looked more like the cute and perky cheerleaders in high school who only went for the Todd Redding types.

Besides, nothing could become of a relationship between them. Clay was determined to leave small-town life as quickly as he could, while Megan clearly belonged in a place like Brighton Valley. And for a man who'd finally made it in the real world, he'd best remind his libido of that simple fact.

It was well after two o'clock by the time Don returned to Zorba's. Clay knew Megan was getting antsy to go pick up her daughter from school and check on Tyler. The woman had been stealing more glances at the clock above the filing cabinets than at the blouse that kept coming undone.

She'd jury-rigged the buttonhole with a bent paper clip, but even the paper clip was having difficulty staying in place.

Luckily, Don's arrival helped defuse the sexual tension that had been building since this morning.

"I'm back," the manager declared as he entered through the back door of the shop. "Now we can get back to work."

Had Don thought that Clay—or rather, Peyton—and Megan had been sitting around the shop playing cards while he'd been gone?

Clay's frustration level with the store manager had reached an all-time high, and it didn't help that his libido was twisted in knots or that he'd spent the past hour discreetly popping antacids, as well as breath mints, because his stomach was a mess, and he could still taste onions and chili and tamale pie.

But something about the way Don looked was even more unsettling than that.

Megan, who'd already reached for her purse a few seconds ago, must have noticed that something wasn't quite right, because her movements stalled.

Clay just about froze in his steps, too.

Don's face had paled dramatically, and beads of perspiration had gathered above his brow.

Megan began to move in reverse. Then she dropped her purse and made her way to the older man's side. "You're looking a bit tired. Can I get you some water or something?"

Her description was an understatement. Don was more than tired. He was about to collapse.

"Sit down," Megan told him.

When Don complied, plopping down in the chair nearest him, she said, "Take some deep breaths."

As he did so, she reached over and rubbed his shoulder.

"I'll be fi..." Don slouched in his chair.

Clay knew he ought to step in and take command of the situation, but Megan seemed to be holding her own.

Hell, she was doing better than that. She appeared to be a natural when it came to handling a crisis. And while he'd had to learn how to do that at a very early age, thanks to dealing with a mom who'd had severe mood swings and other issues, he hadn't had to look out for anyone but himself for so long, it was kind of nice to step back and take a back seat on this one.

That is, until Don's eyes rolled back.

Had he just passed out?

Did Clay need to perform CPR? He was medically trained. But Don appeared to be breathing. Would it be better to call to 911?

"Peyton," Megan said, "help me lower him to the floor so he doesn't fall."

Realizing that was probably the best thing to do, Clay did as she asked. After Megan slipped her hand under her boss's head, they maneuvered the man's body to the floor.

Then, kneeling beside him, they tried to arrange him in a more comfortable position.

Since Don was still breathing, CPR wasn't needed. But a call for paramedics definitely was.

Megan placed her left fingers on Don's neck along with her right hand. She held them there for only a moment, then reached across to Clay's waistline and unclipped his cell phone from his belt.

He nearly jumped as her fingers skimmed his stomach, but his adrenaline really shot through the roof when he realized that his smartphone, which she now held, contained all of his personal information—and nothing of Peyton Johnson's.

He thought about snatching the phone out of her hands to make the call himself—before she was able to scroll through his files and find out who he really was. But Don's moan reminded him that they were in an emergency situation and that a potentially dying man was a million times more important than his stupid secret identity.

"This is Megan Adams," she said to the 911 operator, her voice calm and in control. "I'm at Zorba the Geek's Computer Repair Shop at 293 Main Street in Brighton Valley. My boss just collapsed. We need an ambulance immediately."

Don moaned again, and Clay spoke to him in a soft, steady voice. "You're going to be okay, Don. Megan is calling an ambulance for you. We'll make sure we get you to the hospital in no time."

In what seemed like ages but was probably only a couple of minutes a siren sounded and grew louder. Clay had to give Brighton Valley's first responders kudos for getting here so quickly.

Two paramedics and three firefighters came in through the front door and Megan waved the emergency personnel into the back room.

"He came into the shop about four minutes ago," Megan said, impressing Clay with the way she'd kept her head and her senses during the emergency. "He was extremely pale and seemed kind of shaky. He made it to his desk chair and sat down about forty-five seconds before he collapsed."

One of the paramedics began taking Don's vital signs while the other fired off medical-history questions at Megan.

"I know he takes blood pressure medicine and has

high cholesterol," she said. "His family has a history of diabetes, but as far as I know, he's never been checked."

"Are you family?" one of the female firefighters asked Clay.

"Uh, no. I just work here. His wife is…" Clay looked again to Megan for direction. He knew the woman's name was Cindy, but Megan would know more about how to get in touch with her and who should do it. This was probably the last thing anyone undergoing chemo should have to worry about.

Megan swooped in with the proper answer, just as he'd figured she would.

Again, he had to give her credit for keeping her head, for maintaining her control. She'd been a model of perfection—well, except for those two buttons that had come undone again. He didn't blame her for not noticing, but the male paramedic kneeling down at eye level with her chest did.

The guy, who was probably in his early thirties and looked as if he could bench-press a gurney, flashed a smile at Megan—a smile that looked way more flirtatious than reassuring.

Clay didn't like it.

"So are you going to ride along to the hospital with him?" the leering paramedic asked her as he stole another glance down her shirt.

Okay, so maybe he wasn't leering, but he was definitely taking advantage of the beautiful display of womanhood. And while Clay hadn't been able to help doing the same thing, he wasn't going to cut the guy any slack when he was supposed to be a trained professional, which meant he was way out of line.

Megan looked at the clock, and Clay blurted out,

"No, she can't go. She has to pick up her kids from school. I'll ride to the hospital with him."

Megan looked at him in question, but hell. Clay had sat by idly for the past several minutes. It was time for him to take the situation into control. He hadn't earned the right to be called boss or CEO for nothing.

"Close up the shop," he told Megan. "And put a sign in the window saying we'll reopen tomorrow. Then go get your kids. On your way, call Mrs. Carpenter and whoever else you need to notify. Let them know what happened and where he's going. I'll stay with him at the hospital until someone from his family can get there and take over. Call me if you have any problems."

Megan, who'd taken charge just moments ago, nodded, passing on the leadership baton without question.

Clay then turned to the paramedics, who'd just secured Don onto the gurney. "Okay, let's go."

The firefighters left, no longer needed now that the paramedics had their patient secured. The good-looking male turned back to Megan as if to tell her goodbye.

Or maybe he'd been tempted to ask for her number. Who knew what handsome, muscle-bound guys like that did when it came to making moves on women like Megan?

Clay had struggled with self-confidence when he'd been a teenager. And while he'd ditched those old insecurities when he'd earned his first million and had finally grown up and filled out, being undercover in Brighton Valley seemed to have brought that scrawny, geeky side back in a rush.

That, of course, was another reason for him to get things worked out at the store, hire new employees if need be and then leave town for good.

As Clay followed the gurney to the front of the store, Megan had already scrawled out a note and was placing it on the front door, oblivious to the paramedic's interest in her and her endowments.

But the guy was busy now, too, getting Don loaded into the ambulance. Once the gurney was secured in the back, Clay climbed in and took a seat near Don's head.

The ambulance took off, the shrill sound of the siren letting the other cars on the road know they needed to pull over.

"I'm going to get an IV started on him," the female paramedic said. "He's dehydrated. Besides, they might need to administer meds when we get him to the hospital, so this will speed things up."

Clay nodded, glad that the stud muffin was the one driving so Clay wouldn't be forced to put him in his place. There wasn't anything professional about checking out single mothers when a man ought to be doing his job.

Heck, maybe Clay would even benefit from that conversation. He knew he'd been guilty of the exact same thing, but that was different.

The ride to the medical center took less than five minutes, and as the hospital personnel rushed into action, Clay was handed a plastic bag with Don's personal effects and then told to take a seat in the waiting room.

He'd hardly had a chance to find an empty chair when a tall woman with a headful of tiny braids, a pearly-white smile and Mickey Mouse scrubs introduced herself as LaRonda, the admissions clerk. Clay followed her to a small desk. After taking a seat, he opened up Don's wallet to get the man's driver's license and insurance card.

As LaRonda keyed in the needed information Clay was able to now provide, Clay noticed a few pictures tucked into the wallet. He felt like a voyeur looking at someone else's personal effects, but what else was he supposed to do while he sat there?

"I just love Don," LaRonda said as she continued to enter data into the computer.

The medical center probably taught their personnel to make small talk with scared family members, but Clay couldn't really respond. In fact, he felt like a fraud sitting here because he really didn't know the man at all.

"His wife Cindy is in here all the time," LaRonda continued. "And you'll never see a more loving husband. My stars, how he dotes on his wife."

As Clay glanced at Don's wallet, looking for anything that should be reported to the doctors or the staff, he spotted a picture of what appeared to be a wedding photo of a much younger, much thinner Don and a smiling bride he assumed was Cindy. The next picture was a shot of the two of them on the beach, arms wrapped around each other, with three little kids playing in the sand. The third picture was definitely more recent and showed Cindy holding a sign that said Happy 65th Birthday! Let's Drive into Our Retirement Sunset! She was standing in front of a motor home that was decorated with a bright red bow.

The next slot didn't hold a picture. It held a business card for a local oncologist that had Cindy's name written on the front along with the time of her next chemo appointment.

A sense of dread settled into Clay's stomach. Instead of embarking on their retirement dream, Don was nursing his wife through cancer. He wondered if the couple had ever had time to embark on any trips in that new motor home. Judging by the birth date listing Don as four months past his sixty-fifth birthday, Clay doubted it.

"Uh-oh." LaRonda squinted at her screen and moved her reading glasses to the top of her braided hair.

"What?" Clay didn't like where this was heading.

"It looks like the Carpenters have exhausted their insurance limits for the year because of Cindy's treatments. That chemo can get real expensive."

"So you're saying the insurance won't cover Don's medical bills?" Clay wondered what kind of low-budget rinky-dink insurance policy the Carpenters had. "Who's their insurance provider?"

LaRonda told Clay the name of his own insurance company and added, "It looks like his employer only provides the basics."

Clay cringed at the implication. Geekon was a multi-billion-dollar industry, and while Clay knew he couldn't be held accountable for every HR decision, he found it appalling that his company hadn't provided better for its employees. Some heads back at corporate were going to roll when Clay got done with them.

"Don't worry about the extra cost," he told LaRonda. "I'm a corporate accountant for Zorba the Geek's, and the company will pick up the costs of Mr. Carpenter's hospital bill. We'll pick up the excess of Cindy's treatments, too."

He reached for his phone. He had to tell Zoe to expect a call from the Brighton Valley Medical Center and to set up a meeting with whoever was responsible for purchasing the company's health-care policy. But his phone wasn't clipped to his belt. Where had he used it last?

Then he realized Megan must still have it since she'd used it to call 911.

Dammit. He needed to get it back before his whole undercover identity got blown to pieces.

Chapter Six

Megan found a parking spot near the entrance to the emergency room and pulled her car into the tight space. Before climbing out and locking the doors, she grabbed a lightweight navy blue cardigan she'd intended to drop off at the dry cleaner and slipped it on, buttoning it up as she walked toward the hospital entrance.

There was no way she'd run around town in the green shirt that kept popping buttons, but she hadn't wanted to take time to go home and change clothes, especially since Sam and Caroline had offered to drive Lisa to the house, where Tyler was, and watch both kids there.

She knew that she probably wasn't needed at the hospital, but she couldn't help worrying about Don. Besides, Peyton was going to need a ride back to the shop. And besides that, she had to give him back his cell phone, which had been vibrating almost nonstop since he'd left without it.

Amid all the chaos surrounding the 911 call, she'd neglected to return it before he'd taken off with Don in the ambulance. And judging by the way the display screen kept lighting up with "Call From Zoe," she feared he was missing some pretty important calls.

As she entered the medical center through the automatic doors, she again checked to make sure her cardigan was buttoned to the very top. After the display of lace and skin she'd been showing off all day, she was tempted to stay covered up until winter.

She made her way to the information desk and told the volunteer that she was looking for Don Carpenter.

The older woman clicked away on her computer before turning to Megan with a smile. "He's on the second floor—in room two eighteen."

That meant he'd been admitted. But at least he wasn't in the ICU. That was good, wasn't it?

Megan thanked the woman, then headed toward the elevator just as Peyton's cell phone again buzzed in her pants pocket.

Up until now, she'd been trying her best to ignore it, but on the outside chance that the call was a work-related emergency, she thought it might be a good idea to check and see. After all, she was a Zorba's employee, too. Maybe the powers that be in the corporate office would realize that the people working at the Brighton Valley store were able to handle a crisis.

She pulled out the cell phone and glanced at the lighted display, noting that instead of a phone call, he'd received a text from someone named Collette. She meant to ignore it, but her finger slipped on the touch screen, and the white text box shot to life.

I'll be flying in tonight. Dinner? Drinks? Or something else…?

Okay, so that certainly wasn't a work-related message.

As the elevator doors sprung open, her stomach tightened, and heat spread up her neck and cheeks. The last thing she needed was for Peyton to catch her reading his private messages. So she thrust the offending cell phone back into her pocket.

Yet the warmth in her face didn't disperse—nor did the knot that had formed in her tummy the moment she realized a woman wanted Peyton to join her for dinner or drinks—or *whatever*.

Surely her reaction had nothing to do with jealousy. After all, what did she care if he was seeing a woman who sounded like a…a…French bimbo?

Okay, so maybe there was a small smidgen of green-eyed something or other going on inside. But there certainly *shouldn't* be.

Two nurses rushed by, pushing a cart holding an array of computerized medical equipment, which reminded her of where she was and why she was here. She'd come to check on Don. Nothing else mattered.

As she rounded the corner toward room 218, she pulled up short when she spotted Peyton standing outside talking to a pregnant woman in a white lab coat. Megan recognized her as Dr. Betsy Nielson, the E.R. doctor who'd treated Tyler's broken arm when he'd fallen from the peach tree last summer.

Dr. Nielson was married to Jason Alvarez, although she'd kept her own name.

Peyton ran a hand through his hair, and as much as Megan hated to admit it, he looked just as sexy as ever, causing a tingle to start in her core.

Wait. That wasn't a tingle. It was a vibrating phone.

She pulled the ringing cell from her pocket, then crossed the hall and joined him and the doctor. "Excuse me," she said, as she thrust the phone at him, wanting to get rid of it.

And maybe to get rid of him, too.

As Peyton excused himself and stepped aside to take the call, Megan asked the doctor, "How's Don Carpenter doing?"

"He's resting. We have him hooked up to an IV, and I've run some preliminary tests."

"Was it a heart attack or a stroke?"

"I don't think so. But we're still evaluating him."

"Will he be all right?"

"He's stable."

"Good." Megan shot a glance at Peyton, watched him scan his missed-calls list. At least he was polite enough not to take that phone call in the middle of a busy hospital wing.

"The EKG doesn't show signs of trauma," Dr. Nielson said, "but we're still waiting for his blood work."

"Have you talked to his wife?" Megan had called Cindy earlier to let her know what was going on, but there hadn't been an answer. She assumed the woman was resting and knew she was too ill to drive to the hospital on her own.

"Yes, Mr. Johnson got her number from the patient when he was a bit more lucid. I spoke to her and let her know what was going on. I also called her oncologist just so he'd know what she was dealing with. She plans to have her neighbor bring her over first thing in the morning. Plus, when Mr. Carpenter wakes up tonight, his assigned nurse can help him call home. In the meantime, it's best if we let him get all the rest he can."

"Thank you so much, Dr. Nielson."

"According to Mr. Johnson, Don should be thanking you. He said you acted very quickly and were in control of the situation the entire time. Don is lucky he has someone like you working for him at the shop. Oh, and speaking of Zorba's, Mayor Mendez told my husband about the one-day sale you're having on laptops. My husband stopped by the shop, but it was closed. Now I realize why. But is the deal still available online? I wanted to get one as a gift for my niece. She'll be going off to college in the fall."

"I'm not sure, but Peyton has a contact in the corporate office. Her name is Zoe. She's the one who approved of the initial sale. While I had his cell phone, her number popped up numerous times today, so I have it memorized."

After Megan provided Zoe's contact information, Dr. Nielson thanked her and headed back to the E.R. just as Peyton returned from scanning his phone and checking his messages.

Megan couldn't help but wonder if he'd texted Collette—and if so, what he'd told her.

Peyton merely stared at her. By the way he was biting on the inside of his cheek, he looked as though he wanted to say something.

"So it appears that Don is okay," Megan said. "At least for now."

"Um. Yeah."

Why was he looking at her that way? Was he upset that she'd accidentally kept his cell phone? Did he realize she'd read Collette's text?

"They're going to keep him here for a couple of days," Peyton added. "Then he'll have to be off for at least a week so he can recuperate at home. But I'll stick around and help out. I'd hate to leave you to man the shop all on your own."

That meant they'd be working together—just the two of them. And for longer than she'd expected.

But there were more important things to worry about.

"Poor Don," she said. "He really needs this job. You don't think he'll get fired for taking too much time off, do you?"

Peyton touched his nose again. He had this funny habit of running his index finger along the bridge of his nose as if he were pushing a pair of glasses back in place, even though he didn't wear them. She'd noticed him doing it several times, and she found it kind of quirky—but cute.

When he caught her watching him, he shoved his hands into his pockets. "I don't think he'll get fired— or suffer too much financially by being off work. The company has a sunshine fund set up for situations like this. Plus, now it makes sense why things were going downhill over th… I mean, why we… Oh heck, you know what I'm trying to say. It just all makes more sense now. And I'm sure the corporate office will work with Don until he gets back on his feet and is able to take over running the store again."

"Hmm."

"Hmm, what?" Peyton asked.

"Hmm, we'll see about that. I've never really trusted big corporations. I'm a small-town girl. Everyone looks out for each other here. But out there?" Megan gestured toward the window that looked out at the big, wide world. "Companies like Geekon Enterprises don't really look out for the little people. That's why I've been so stressed about having you here. I worried you'd report back to them and tell them that Don and I needed to be replaced."

Megan hadn't meant to voice her fears out loud, but the adrenaline dump had kicked in, and she wondered if her and Peyton becoming a team during the emergency had made her feel more comfortable with him.

"What exactly would there be to report?" he asked.

"Oh, you know. That Mr. Carpenter has been a little scattered, that he's had to take a lot of time off lately, that the paperwork isn't organized. That he should be let go. But he really needs this job, as well as the medical insurance, even though it's a pretty low-rate plan."

Peyton tensed.

"I don't mean to sound disloyal," she said. "I'm sure Don is thrilled to have health insurance through the company. But just between you and me, it's only going to cover the cost of Cindy's basic treatments."

"I hear that the plan is going to improve—and that their coverage is better than they thought."

"I hope you're right." She offered him a smile. "Please don't say anything to anyone back at the corporate office. I need my job, too. And while the shop hasn't been running smoothly for a while, I'm trying to fix things. And now that you're helping me get the new accounting system in place, everything should be back to normal soon—especially when Don gets off bed rest."

Judging from the furrowed line between Peyton's brows, Megan suspected that she'd unloaded way too much on the poor man. But goodness, what a relief it was to finally get it off her chest and to no longer feel as though she had to hide anything.

"I'll make a few calls. I'm sure no one will lose their job over this. Besides, between the two of us, we can get the shop back in shape before Don gets back. That should make the big guys over at corporate take notice, right?"

Megan appreciated Peyton's attempt to console her. Maybe he really was on her and Don's side. She still didn't trust corporations, though. But maybe she could trust him.

"That's sweet of you to offer, Peyton." She placed a hand on his arm, felt the corded muscles tense under her fingers, felt the heat of his body.

He looked down to where her hand rested on his arm, and she withdrew her fingers immediately.

She hadn't meant to get so touchy-feely, especially since it appeared that he was taken.

Or that Collette certainly wanted him to be taken.

"Uh, is there a cab company or something in this town that I can call? I rode in the ambulance here and don't have a way to get back to the shop."

"Oh, my gosh! Of course. That's another reason I'm here. I planned to give you a ride. Just let me go peek in on Don before we leave."

"Okay, thanks. I have to make a few calls, so I'll be over here in the waiting area."

Megan remembered all those missed calls. "Oh, by

the way, Zoe has been trying to reach you. I didn't want to answer your phone. But after talking to Dr. Nielson, maybe I should have. I told everyone in the diner today about the sale on laptops, and since we had to close the shop down, Zoe has probably been getting a ton of calls."

Peyton scrunched his face as if he'd just caught a whiff of a dirty bedpan.

"But don't worry, Peyton. I'm sure she processed those orders from everyone who called and gave you credit for them. Just think, with that kind of boost in sales, those corporate bigwigs at Geekon might see you as more than just an accountant. They might even give you a promotion."

"Lucky me," Peyton said. "I might end up owning the company."

Megan laughed. Imagine that. Peyton as the CEO. She'd never seen a picture of Clayton Jenkins, nor did she know anything about the man. But she could imagine what he'd be like if she ever did cross paths with him—too smart and greedy and highfalutin for his own good.

Clay stood in the hallway, his cell phone in hand, and watched Megan enter Don's room. She was still chuckling over the thought of Peyton Johnson heading up the company someday, so he assumed she hadn't uncovered his identity yet.

Apparently, Megan might be a beautiful, nurturing woman, but she wasn't a snoop. He couldn't say that about a lot of people who knew that he was actually Clay Jenkins, the CEO of Geekon Enterprises.

And he had to admit, if he were to make a note of Megan's admirable qualities, the list would be growing.

While she checked in on Don, Clay walked into the empty second-floor waiting room to call Zoe.

His efficient executive assistant picked up on the first ring. "What in the world is going on over there?"

Had she already heard about Don's collapse? He'd planned to inform her, but without his cell phone, he hadn't been able to do so yet. Maybe LaRonda, the admissions clerk, had already contacted the home office and they'd alerted her.

"Don Carpenter, the manager of the Brighton Valley store, was rushed to the hospital," he said. "The doctors are still examining him, so I don't know any more than that right now."

"I'm sorry, Clay. I didn't mean to jump you the moment the phone rang, but I've been fielding calls right and left about the special promotion you've been offering all the locals. Caroline Jennings, who owns a diner, got my name from Megan Adams, the woman you had me talk to. Since the Brighton Valley store is closed, and Caroline wasn't sure how long that sale was going on, she called me at the Houston office to order two computers. And she's not the only one. Apparently everyone else in town wanted to take advantage of that special price, too. So she's been passing out my contact information."

"How many calls have you received?"

"I've lost count."

"Sorry about that. I forgot how quickly word spreads in a small town. And since I rode to the medical center with Don, I've been out of the loop."

"I know. Ray Mendez, the mayor, told me that Mr. Carpenter was taken to the hospital in an ambulance."

"The *mayor* told you? How did he know about Don?"

"He'd talked to Caroline earlier, and she gave him my number. He placed an order for three laptops—two for city hall and one for his home. Then, after stopping by someplace called the Stagecoach Inn, where he met the E.R. doctor's husband, he found out about Mr. Carpenter."

"I had no idea—"

"You didn't? At a hundred dollars a pop for that laptop? In the last two hours, I've talked to more people in that little town than you probably did in all the time you lived there."

Clay had never told anyone, especially those who knew him now, about his shy, awkward and painful teenage years. But Zoe was probably right.

He ran a hand through his hair, mentally calculating how much profit he had blown by making that offer to Riley yesterday. Maybe he should've stuck with Megan's cookie idea.

"Did you approve the sale for everyone who called?" he asked.

"Sure did. That's what you asked me to do, wasn't it? And so far I've put through all thirty-two orders."

"Oh, wow."

"I tried to call you to double-check, but you didn't answer your phone. So I just rolled with the plan you'd set in motion."

"No, you did the right thing. In the chaos of the 911 call and everything, Megan used my cell phone. She's had it while I've been at the hospital."

"So then she must have seen that Collette's been hot on your trail this afternoon, too."

Crap. Clay had forgotten about the text from Collette. He hoped Megan wasn't nosy enough to read his messages. Or maybe she wouldn't even care that another woman was sending him sexy invitations to reignite a relationship that had fizzled out months ago. But he'd need to deal with the supermodel before she became a problem.

"What did you tell Collette?" Clay asked, even though his assistant was the epitome of discretion and was under strict instructions not to divulge his whereabouts to anyone.

"I stalled her for the time being. But you know how she is. If you don't call her back yourself, she'll be in the office first thing tomorrow morning, paparazzi trailing behind her, demanding to know where you are."

Zoe hit the nail on the head. As usual. Clay had first met the world-famous Collette d'Ante at a black-tie fund-raiser where he'd been the guest of honor. She'd moved in swiftly, letting him know she'd like to be more than a casual acquaintance.

He'd never had such a beautiful woman hit on him, and when she asked him out for an intimate dinner later that week, he'd agreed.

Collette had implied that she hated the fame and attention her career had attracted, and he'd thought he'd found a kindred spirit since he was on his own quest for financial success with social anonymity.

But when the paparazzi showed up at every restaurant or event they attended, no matter what he did to circumvent them, he realized they were being tipped off. And shortly thereafter, he'd realized that Collette, who made such sweet claims, hadn't meant any of them. So he'd ended things with her before she got any ideas about becoming the first Mrs. Geekon Enterprises.

But apparently, she was under the impression that absence really did make the heart grow fonder, which wasn't true in Clay's case. She was too self-absorbed and way more trouble than she was worth.

And as Zoe had said, if he didn't call her himself and tell her that *it's over* meant over for good, she'd have every tabloid wolfhound scenting him out by tomorrow afternoon.

"I'll deal with Collette. You handle the rest of the Brighton Valley laptop orders. I'll cover the difference out of my own pocket. But no more sales after today."

"Will you also cover the difference for all the overtime I'm going to make taking these calls tonight?"

"Zoe, you don't get overtime. You're on salary—and a very generous one, at that."

"Okay, then you can just put it on my Fourth of July bonus check."

"You don't get a Fourth of—"

"Sorry, boss. There's a call on the other line—no doubt with another laptop order coming in. Gotta go."

The line disconnected before Clay could tell Zoe he also wanted to schedule a meeting with the person in charge of the company health-insurance plans. Oh, well, that would have to wait until tomorrow.

At the sound of shoes clicking upon the tiled hospital floor, he looked up to see Megan coming his way, her back straight and her chin up. Yet there was a lingering tension in her shoulders. This had to have been a stressful day for her.

Was she still afraid the corporate office would find

out about Don's failures and the store's financial situation?

He wanted to rub those shoulders and tell her everything was going to be all right, that he'd make sure of it.

The smile she shot him was sweet and genuine, even if it was a little tired. "Ready?"

He was more than ready and wanted to tell her so, but he thought better of it. She was just offering to give him a ride back to the shop because she knew he was stranded—and because she was a nurturer. What else did he expect from a woman like her?

"Yep, all set." He pocketed his phone and raised his arms up to stretch out his own shoulders and back.

Man, he could use a good run right now. And then a hot meal and a long sleep.

As they walked toward the elevator, an orderly turned the corner pushing an empty bed, and Clay instinctively reached out and wrapped his hand around Megan's waist to pull her to the opposite side of the hallway.

She pressed into his side to allow the gurney room to pass. It seemed only natural to let his hand linger on her waist as they continued to the elevator door, his fingers resting along the curve of her hip.

She wore a blue sweater now. Underneath, was she still wearing the green blouse with the buttons that popped open?

It would be so easy to slip his hand underneath that blue woven fabric to feel for the green top that had given him such a lovely view earlier today.

When she leaned forward to push the call button, their bodies broke free from each other, which was for the best. If they were going to have to work alone together for the next week or so, he'd need to keep his hands and his eyes to himself.

They took the elevator to the lobby, where the after-work crowd had begun to stream into the hospital for visiting hours.

"If you haven't picked up groceries yet for the apartment, I can stop at the market on the way back so you'll have something to eat."

"Don't worry about me. You probably need to get home to your kids and feed them."

"Actually, my kids are with Caroline. She watches them for me whenever I need a sitter. I called earlier, and she's probably already fed them."

"Have you had dinner yet?" Clay asked, trying to sound casual, as though he was merely asking her if she'd done the biology homework last night.

He didn't want her to think he was asking her out on a date. Yet, more importantly, he didn't want her to turn him down.

As they walked through the sliding glass doors and into the parking lot, he reached up to push his nonexistent glasses back up his nose before he remembered he wasn't in high school anymore.

Hell, he had Collette d'Ante chasing after him, wanting to re-create some kind of relationship for all the world to see, but here he was, stumbling over his own feet in his attempt to get Megan to join him for dinner.

"No, I've been too worried about Don to eat anything. The hospital cafeteria is probably still open, if you want to go back in there."

Clay had spent enough time in hospitals when he was a kid and his mother had bounced in and out of mental institutions. He tried to avoid them as much as possible, especially the cafeterias.

"Or we could stop by the Tastee Cone before I drop you off back at Zorba's."

Now, that was a blast from the past. The Tastee Cone, which was located between Brighton Valley and Wexler, had been the only fast-food joint around. So by default it was the hangout of choice for the local teenagers who had a few extra allowance dollars burning a hole in their pockets.

Clay had always enjoyed their food, but he'd never parked in the lot with the cool kids and their tricked-out cars and lifted trucks, blasting music, flirting with each other and chatting about who was taking who to homecoming.

"That sounds good," he said. "But can we just eat there? I really don't want to take anything to go."

The truth was, Clay actually wanted to experience the Tastee Cone for once—just as all the popular kids had done back in the day. He wanted to sit out in the parking lot with a beautiful girl—who, he was willing to bet his Geekon trademark, had once been a cheerleader. And he wanted to drink an orange cream milkshake, listen to music and not have to worry about some football captain smashing a chocolate-dipped cone into his forehead, which was what had happened last time he'd braved the Tastee Cone during prime time.

"Sure," she said as she popped the locks open on her car and they got in. "But that place can be crawling with teenagers, especially since today was the last day of school before summer vacation. There'll be lots of music and revving of engines and all the stuff small-town kids do to show off in front of each other."

Clay was counting on it. That's what he'd missed in high school. And sweet, beautiful Megan would be right by his side.

As they drove down the rural highway that connected the two towns, he could almost imagine her in a cheerleader uniform, doing backflips, shaking her pom-poms....

They turned into the driveway entrance, and she pulled her car up to one of the covered parking spaces, where they could place their orders through the old-fashioned speaker system that was stationed at every other parking spot.

A couple of boys in the car next to them honked and yelled out to three girls who wore Brighton Valley High Pep Squad T-shirts.

"This place reminds me of high school," Megan said.

"I have to ask," Clay said. "Were you a cheerleader?"

She stared at him for a moment, her brow slightly scrunched as if wondering why he'd ask, why it would even matter.

"Yes," she finally said. "How'd you know?"

He'd crushed after the type long enough that he could just tell. But he didn't dare admit it to her. Instead he smiled and said, "I don't know. It was just a guess."

She seemed to stew on that for a moment, as though she wasn't sure if she should take his assessment as a compliment or not. So he tried to brush it all aside by moving on to something safer. "What do you want to eat?"

Megan ordered a grilled chicken sandwich and an unsweetened iced tea, while Clay chose the Double Tastee Burger, fries and an orange cream shake.

"Did you grow up around here?" he asked.

"No, I actually grew up outside of Houston, but when my dad died, my mom moved me and my younger brother back here to live with Gram out at her orchard. I transferred to Brighton Valley High my sophomore year."

"Did you like school?" Clay figured she must have. The popular kids usually did. It was those who hadn't fit in who'd struggled with attendance.

"It was okay, I guess. I liked the social aspects. But when I was in elementary school, I was diagnosed with dyslexia. So I hated it back then."

"You seem to have overcome your disability," he said.

"Yes, for the most part—and with time and the learning lab at the high school. But when I was Lisa's age, money was tight for our family and there was never any extra for tutoring. That's why I'm determined to provide the help she needs. And the extra hours I work at Zorba's is one way I can afford to do that."

Thank goodness he hadn't followed his gut and fired her when he'd first arrived.

A waitress on roller skates brought out their order and Clay reached for his wallet while Megan protested. "Nope, you bought lunch today. Dinner is on me."

Then, after picking up the tab, she laid out napkins and ketchup packets and put the straw in his milkshake—just as she would have done for one of her kids. Somehow it made him feel taken care of. Doted on.

He bit into his double cheeseburger, which tasted better than anything in the world, simply because this particular beautiful woman sat next to him, and he finally belonged.

At least the guy pretending to be Peyton Johnson belonged. Clay didn't know where *he* fit in, but he would just enjoy the juicy burger, the gorgeous redhead and the curious—maybe even envious—stares from the teenagers around him.

"So you've lived in Brighton Valley ever since high school?" Clay asked, wanting to know more about her.

"No, actually I came back after my divorce. And now that I'm here, I don't ever intend to leave."

"Going away was a bad experience?"

"You could say that. The entire marriage was a bad experience. But I only have myself to blame."

"Do you want to talk about it?"

"No, not really. Let's just say it was a blessed mistake and an unfortunate learning experience."

When he looked at her in confusion, she went on. "I love Tyler more than life itself, but let's just say that he came a little too early."

"Ah. I see." And Clay actually did. His friend Rick had gotten his girlfriend, Mallory, pregnant back in high school. It had ended well for them—they'd finally reunited ten years after the fact. But there'd been a lot of hard lessons and rough patches along the way.

"Mine is a classic story," Megan said. "Good-girl cheerleader dates captain of the football team and ends up pregnant. Football Captain grudgingly marries Cheerleader because his rich granddaddy says he has to. Cheerleader gives marriage her best try but Football Captain can't commit and leaves her and their two kids for a wealthy cougar. Then Football Captain and Cougar ride off into the sunset in her white Mercedes, never to be heard from again. That's my marital experience in a nutshell."

Megan took a bite of her grilled chicken sandwich and nodded toward the pep-squad girls, who by now had been convinced to join the rowdy boys sitting on the tailgate of the truck next to them.

"See those girls? Every time I come here, I just want to grab each of them by their shoulders, shake them and tell them not to settle for some boy who drives a truck and can score a touchdown every Friday night. A few whistles and catcalls do not equal love."

"What about those poor unsuspecting boys whose hormones are changing every day? They're probably nervous as hell around those girls, so they puff up like roosters walking through a henhouse because they don't know how else to get a female's attention."

"Those boys will be just fine. They'll learn to lie and sneak around and cheat on their spouses soon enough."

"Wait, you can't think that all men are like your ex-husband." Oh, boy. Football Captain had sure done a number on her. Clay wanted to punch the no-good lying jerk who'd done her wrong like that. He hated liars even more than he hated football players—at least, those who were bullies like Todd Redding and his buddies.

"No," Megan said. "I realize all men aren't like my ex-husband. My grandpa certainly wasn't. And my dad adored my mother. There are plenty of trustworthy men in town. Unfortunately, I seem to be a magnet for the liars."

She attracted liars? More than one? Who else had lied to her or let her down?

"How's your shake, Peyton?"

Peyton...?

Oh, no. It wasn't like that. He wasn't a liar. He was just protecting his identity. Once he got the store turned around, which should be soon, he would tell her who he really was. Maybe then she wouldn't be so distrustful of men or the folks in the corporate office.

Or of him.

Chapter Seven

Megan couldn't believe how much she and Peyton had gotten done in almost a week. Of course, now that school was out, she actually had more time to work because the kids were enrolled in a summer day camp as well as an enrichment program, which kept them busy most of the day.

In addition, she was finally getting the hang of the new accounting system Peyton had installed. Don, who was recovering at home, would be surprised to find out how much they'd accomplished.

After running a series of tests, the doctors at the Brighton Valley Medical Center had decided that Don had been suffering from exhaustion. They discharged him five days ago, and he was now recuperating at home with strict orders to take it easy.

Last night when Megan stopped by his house to visit

him and Cindy, they told her someone from the corporate office had called. Just as Peyton had thought, there really was a sunshine fund that would see them through their present financial problems. And apparently, their insurance plan had an emergency clause that would kick in and cover all the excess hospital and medical bills for both Don's hospitalization and Cindy's treatments, which was a real godsend.

It would still be another week before Don would be able to return to work, though. But that was okay. Thanks to Peyton's help, Megan was no longer adrift in a river of invoices and customer complaints.

In fact, Zorba's was finally showing signs of getting back in order. And Peyton, who'd promised to stick around until after Don came back to work, had been a man of his word.

There'd been moments when Megan would catch herself staring at him while he rearranged the shelves. And there were times when he'd come along behind her chair to point out something about how the new system worked. She'd catch a whiff of that amazing aftershave he wore, that clean, woodsy scent that set her senses reeling. Then he'd place his hand over hers as it rested on the mouse, letting it linger longer than necessary. Or maybe it had just felt that way.

Yet there seemed to be a mutual understanding that they needed to behave like professionals and place their attraction on the back burner.

The problem was Megan wasn't sure how much her back burner could hold before the attraction pot boiled over.

She'd originally thought Peyton would be here for only a couple of days. And even though she'd both appreciated and needed his assistance, the bookkeeping system was well in place and there wasn't really much left for an accountant to do around here.

Yesterday he'd started working on some of the computer repairs to help Don catch up, which was really helpful, but she was a little concerned about that, too. After all, she wasn't sure what kind of training he had. What if he wasn't able to fix things properly?

The customers all knew about Don's illness now, so they would be more understanding about the delay in getting their computers back. And since many of them had purchased new laptops, there wasn't much for them to complain about.

If truth be told, it would be best if Peyton went back to the city. Best for her, anyway, because as much as she intended to keep a professional air about her while the two of them worked together, it was getting more and more difficult to do, especially if he insisted upon wearing that blasted aftershave and peering over her shoulder to look at her screen while she worked.

"How's it going?" he asked as he bent over her desk again, setting off a flurry of pheromones and a bevy of goose bumps chasing up and down her arms.

His face was so close to hers that if she turned to the right, she might actually be close enough to press a kiss on his cheek—if she were so inclined.

"It's going okay."

If he didn't step away, she was going to have to ask what brand of cologne he wore. And she wasn't about to do that.

Finally, he must've taken pity on her because he moved over to the shelf of waiting computers. Then he knelt down and reached for the cords of several machines that had gotten tangled together.

Once he was no longer hovering so close, she changed the subject. "You know, I'll bet Zorba's has a computer technician they could send out here to do some of those repairs. Like a loaner employee or someone like that so you don't have to do it."

"I don't mind fixing a few of these just to help get them back to their owners quicker."

At that, she turned toward him and as their gazes met, her heart stalled for a moment, then took off like a quivering arrow.

He smiled, but he also raised a brow at her, as if he expected her to utter a complaint. And the only one she was tempted to mention was the very last thing in the world she'd ever say to him.

"It's not that we don't need your help." She returned his smile. "I mean, I don't know what Don and I would have done without you. But are you really qualified to be doing so many computer repairs?"

His eyebrow rose even higher. "I can handle a few repairs."

"Of course you can." She hadn't meant to insult him, so she stood and walked over to where he knelt by the shelf in order to soothe his ego better. "It's just that you're an accountant and you're really good at what you do. So don't take this the wrong way, but I think you should be trained or certified to be working on the computers."

She sensed he was about to protest, but she cut him off by placing her hand on his upper arm. "Hear me out. If you just do a temporary fix to get these machines operating and we release them to the customers, the problems could still be there. It would be like putting a Band-Aid on after an open-heart surgery. And we wouldn't want to have to refund our clients' money and do all the work over again."

Peyton's face grew red, and she assumed she'd insulted him in spite of her attempt not to. She hadn't meant to imply that there was anything wrong with being an accountant. Gosh, he was sharp and had helped out tremendously. Who knew where she and Don and the store would be if he hadn't come in when he had?

Before she could soften the blow and explain herself better, point out that they couldn't all be computer geniuses, the bell on the door jangled, and Tyler's voice called out, "Hey! Where are you going?"

A bark sounded, followed by thumps and bumps that grew louder and louder upon approaching the back office.

Megan glanced up just as an oversize ball of fur hurled itself toward her. In her squatting position, she fell toward Peyton, causing them both to tumble to the floor in a tangle of limbs and computer cords.

"What in the heck was that?" Clay asked, as he watched the dirty four-legged blur rush up the back steps toward his apartment.

"I think it was a dog." Megan, who just moments ago had set him off by suggesting that he wasn't tech savvy enough to handle some basic computer repairs, now lay on the floor in his arms.

His face—which had warmed with indignation when he'd been sorely tempted to tell her right then and there that he was Clay Jenkins, the one and only founder of

Geekon Enterprises—was now heated by something much different from anger.

With her red hair spilled onto his face and the full, pert breasts he'd spent the past week fantasizing about pressed against his chest, he instinctively wrapped his arms around her to hold her close.

Megan met his gaze, which didn't take any effort since their faces were only inches apart. What could have been desire just moments ago turned to surprise when her son called out, "Pancho," and her daughter's soccer cleats pounded on the floor.

Now what?

"Pancho!" Tyler called out again. "Where'd you go, boy?"

Megan tried to delicately remove herself from her stretched-out position on top of him, but a computer cord caught her ankle, and she was able to get only one leg up, resulting in her straddling his torso. Under any other circumstances, Clay might have actually found the position...nice.

Actually, he found it nice anyway.

"Hey," Tyler said as he entered the back office and spotted the two of them on the floor. "What are you guys doing down there?"

"It's a long story," Clay said, "but if you're looking for a runaway mutt, it just knocked us down before heading upstairs."

"Cool. Thanks. We'll get him." Tyler took off after the mangy dog, as Lisa followed behind.

Clay tried to get up off the floor, but until Megan could roll off the top of him, he wasn't going anywhere.

What a mess. Thank goodness the kids were too busy chasing after "Pancho" to notice the intimate and embarrassing position in which the adults had suddenly found themselves.

"Hold on," Megan said. "My ankle is stuck."

When she reached toward her right foot, the motion brought her into contact with the most male part of his anatomy, and a rush of heat shot up his groin as she tried to reposition herself.

He grabbed her hips to stop her from moving on top of his lap and causing him further arousal, not to mention a bit of embarrassment. He clenched his eyes shut and said, "I'm trying to stay as still as I can, but when you wiggle around like that, it doesn't help."

"But I…" Her movements slowed. "Oh. I'm sorry. I didn't realize…"

What? That he'd been fantasizing about being in this position with her all week? Not that he'd envisioned being on the floor of the shop—or having kids and a dog involved.

The bell on the front door jangled again. With the two kids already accounted for, Clay opened his eyes. Who'd just come in?

Could this situation get any worse?

"We'll be right with you," Megan called out.

Now, how the hell did she expect for that to happen? They were pretty much tied up for the moment. Unless…

Clay sat up to reach the cord on her ankle. He'd pull the damn thing off the monitor if it would get her perfect, compact and sexy body off him any quicker. But his effort merely pushed their torsos closer together, leaving their faces only inches apart.

Megan wrapped her arms around the back of his

shoulders to steady herself just as a gruff but winded male voice sounded from the front of the store.

"I'm sorry, Meggie, but the kids took off after that damn dog before I could stop them, and…" Sam Jennings, Caroline's retired husband, stopped short when he spotted Clay with one hand on the sexy single mother's hip, and her legs wrapped around him.

"Whoops. Sorry to interrupt. I could have sworn the kids ran in here." The man tried to look anywhere but at the two of them all twisted up together on the floor in what had to look like a lovers' embrace.

"They ran upstairs," Megan said. "That fool dog knocked us over, and I'm all tangled up with this computer cord. Where did that thing come from, anyway?"

Clay gave the cord a good hard pull and heard it pop off the back of the monitor. Better to have to repair a broken cord than to stay in this awkward position, especially with the retired sheriff eyeballing him as if he'd gotten Megan in this intimate position on purpose.

Not that he hadn't enjoyed it.

As Megan got to her feet, Sam said, "It's a stray that took up residence in the park. Caroline started calling it Pancho after it snuck into the back of the diner and ate what was left of her tamale pie last week."

"Mom," Lisa said, as she raced down the steps. "We saw the dog in the park after Sheriff Sam picked us up from camp. He said we could keep him if we caught him, and Tyler cornered him in the apartment upstairs, so can we keep him? We caught him fair and square."

While Megan had already gotten off the floor, Clay remained seated, waiting for his arousal to subside a bit more.

"I'm sorry for making that kind of promise to the

kids," Sam said. "I didn't think they'd be able to catch him. The whole town has been after that darn dog for almost two weeks, and he's avoided every last one of us."

At that moment, Tyler came downstairs. "Please, Mom, please. We'll take care of him, I promise."

Clay watched the emotions pass across Megan's face, from embarrassment to annoyance to love. He suspected she was about to give in.

"Where is Pancho now?" she asked.

"I locked him in Mr. Johnson's bedroom. He peed a little bit on the bed, but only because he was so excited. I can train him not to do that in the house, I promise."

"Maybe we should call Dr. Martinez. It wouldn't hurt to ask the vet if anyone is looking for a lost pet. And if not, maybe we should have him examined. If he's been a stray very long, he could be sick or need a flea bath."

At the mention of Rick Martinez, Clay's old friend from high school, he realized he'd better try to contact him again. Rick was the one person in town who would definitely recognize him, which was why Clay had called the veterinary clinic before he'd reached city limits. But Rick's receptionist had said Dr. Martinez had taken his family on vacation to Hawaii.

"Say," Sam said, looking Clay up and down, "is this your first time to Brighton Valley? I could swear I've seen you in town before. And after thirty-plus years on the job, I never forget a face."

Uh-oh. Maybe Rick wasn't the only one.

Megan swooped in to save Clay from telling an out-and-out lie to the retired lawman. "I'm sorry, Sam. This is Peyton Johnson. He's the corporate accountant who was sent from the Houston office." She glanced at Clay. "Isn't that right?"

He smiled, first at her, then at Sam. Using his index finger, he pushed his nonexistent glasses up the bridge of his nose—an unnecessary habit he hoped no one had noticed.

Sam humphed, then nodded toward the door. "Well, now that the kids are home safe and sound, I'll head back to the diner. If you decide not to keep that dog, give Rick Martinez a call anyway. He runs an animal rescue behind his clinic. He'll take him until he can find him a good home."

"He's got a good home with us," Tyler said. "Doesn't he, Mom? Please?"

"All right," she said. "But after you take him out to our car, go back into Mr. Johnson's apartment and make sure you clean up any mess he made."

Both children whooped and cheered, then dashed up the stairs, leaving Clay and Megan alone again.

"You're an easy touch," he said.

She gave a little shrug. "It's just that Tyler's been so withdrawn lately. And this was the first time I've seen him warm up to anyone or anything in a long time. I'm hoping that Pancho will put that happy spark back into my little boy. Know what I mean?"

Clay's first inclination was to say no, but in a way, he supposed he did know what she meant. His mom had had a lot of bad days, but some of them had been good. And on those rare occasions, his life had seemed normal, and he'd actually felt loved. Then, when her mood would swing to one of despair, he would have given anything to see her smile again, to feel her ruffle his hair.

"Yeah," he said, "I know." Then he returned to his

work, only now he had to repair the cord he'd pulled out of the monitor.

If Megan realized how arousing he'd found their tumble to the floor, she didn't let on, and neither did he.

Minutes later, when Tyler returned downstairs with the scrawny stray dog cuddled in his arms, Clay spotted a faint bruise under the boy's left eye that he'd missed seeing before—and a scrape near his right ear. Something told him that chasing after Pancho hadn't caused either injury.

Was someone still picking on the poor kid, even though school was now out and he'd started that enrichment program? If so, that sucked. At least Clay used to get the summers off.

When the kids left the room again, Clay said, "I think that bully still might be bothering Tyler."

Megan glanced up, her lips parted, eyes wide. "How do you know?"

"Just a hunch. When I was a kid, I was small for my age and kids often teased me, too." Like Tyler, Clay had been bright—a genius, actually, although his high IQ had gone unnoticed for a couple of reasons. For one thing, he'd had an undiagnosed vision problem that had made it difficult for him to see the chalkboard in class. And for another, his mom had moved around a lot, making him change schools before anyone could figure out what was wrong.

"But you're not small any longer," Megan said, her gaze skimming over him, caressing him in an appreciative way.

"I grew several inches taller after high school." He'd also gained some weight and begun working out at the gym. With money, success and fame, he'd made some other changes, too—a new longer hair style, designer clothes and eyeglasses. And thanks to some state-of-the-art cosmetic dental work, he had a great smile. Or so he'd been told by some of the beautiful women who clamored to accompany him on his jet-setting lifestyle.

Yet deep inside, there would probably always be a geeky ugly duckling lurking, a kid who'd never had a real home or a place where he fit in.

And it was that kid who found the warmth in Megan's pretty smile a heck of a lot more appealing right now than the smiles of the gushing beauties like Collette who flocked to his side at fancy cocktail parties, eager to tell a rich man anything he wanted to hear.

"If you don't mind," Clay said, "I could take Tyler aside and tell him that I know what it's like to be bullied and tell him that things won't always be like this."

"Kids picked on you?" Megan asked. "That's hard to imagine."

It wouldn't be if she could've seen him back when he'd attended Washington High in nearby Wexler.

"Well, believe me. It got pretty bad at times. I remember one day when I was a freshman in particular. During a pep rally in the gym, some of the football jocks grabbed me, hoisted me up and stuck me in a basketball hoop. Everyone assumed the stunt was part of the performance. Even the teachers laughed as I dangled there, kicking my legs and wondering if humiliation alone could kill a guy."

"That must have been awful for you."

It had been the worst. The star quarterback had been the ringleader. Clay had no idea why, with his popularity, the jock had felt the need to belittle someone to feel even more important than he already was. But he had.

"How long did the teasing go on?" Megan asked.

"Until a couple of new kids came along and put the bully in his place."

Rick Martinez, who was now the Brighton Valley veterinarian, and his brother, Joey, had pretty much been keeping to themselves—until they spotted Todd Redding taunting Clay outside of school one day. When the bullying got physical, and Todd punched Clay, the brothers stepped in. Rick told Todd to back off and to pick on someone his own size.

Never one to back down from a fight, especially on his own turf, Todd left Clay alone so he could shove Rick. A fight broke out, and as was usually the case, Todd came out smelling like a rose—albeit one with a black eye, a split lip and a bloody nose.

The witnesses, all football players, claimed that the new kid had started the fight. Rick, who could have asserted a noble defense, clammed up. He got a three-day suspension for his silent heroism—and Clay's undying loyalty.

An unexpected friendship began that day, and as long as Clay stuck close to Rick, who had a reputation for being a tough street punk, the jocks more or less left him alone.

Todd Redding graduated the following June, which was a big relief. Rumor had it he'd gotten some girl pregnant and had to get married. Good riddance was all Clay could say.

"One of the new kids took a liking to me," Clay said. "And he went so far as to teach me how to defend myself if I ever got into a situation where I couldn't outthink my opponent. If you don't mind, I could show Tyler a few moves. It might help to make him feel better about himself—and to put the bully in his place."

"I've never been one to promote violence, but I can't stand the idea of my son being hurt. I'd certainly appreciate anything you can do to help."

Clay nodded, then went back to work.

Twenty minutes later, as the day drew to a close, and while the kids were cuddled in the corner with Pancho, Megan reached for her purse.

"You know," she said to Clay, "we're not having anything fancy for dinner. Just pot roast and mashed potatoes. But you're welcome to join us—if you'd like to."

The invitation caught him off guard. For one thing, Clay Jenkins, who'd enjoyed meals in some of the fanciest hotels and restaurants in the country, had never eaten dinner on a farm before. But tonight, he couldn't think of a place he'd rather be.

Chapter Eight

Later that evening, Clay looked around the dining room at the quaint farmhouse, with its floral wallpaper, dark oak hutch, and matching table and chairs. He wondered if Megan knew what some of this rustic old furniture would be worth to those hotshot interior designers who were paid a small fortune to make some rich person's second and third homes look exactly like her little family homestead.

In fact, if he hadn't gotten to know her better or didn't understand her shaky financial situation, he'd think that she'd paid a professional to make her house look like a spread in *Southern Living* magazine. But every room in the Adams house was the real deal.

Just as Megan was.

He looked over the enormous platter of pot roast with fingerling potatoes and baby carrots caramelized in the meat juices. She never ceased to amaze him with her talent. And while he'd thought she was beautiful when she worked at Zorba's, here on the farm and in her cozy home, wearing a pair of tight faded jeans and a pink tank top, she was even more so.

Rachael Ray would probably give away her entire line of fancy cookware to look as sexy as Megan did right this second. And to be seated at her table, eating her homemade meal.

Did the kids realize how lucky they were?

Tyler was wolfing down the fresh yeasty rolls, while his sister, Lisa, snuck chunks of the savory beef to Pancho, who hid underneath the table.

"Can I get you some more cabernet?" Megan asked Clay.

"Sure. Thank you." He'd never had a woman cook for him before. He'd always been the one to wine and dine them, especially if he'd wanted to impress them. But Megan, who'd pulled her pretty red hair haphazardly into a ponytail high on her head, her face flushed from the heat of the kitchen, wasn't trying to impress anyone.

Still, she'd snagged Clay's interest in a way no other woman ever had.

His gaze skimmed over her, landing upon a streak of flour that rested right where her snug tank top tapered into her slender waist. And each time she got up from the table to get something else, he couldn't help but watch her move effortlessly about.

There wasn't an ounce of pretense to her, and Clay wished he could be more honest about who he was.

She poured his wine, then added a bit to her own glass. "Can I get you anything else?"

"No, I'm great. Everything's great." And it really

was. Not knowing what else to say, he took a sip of the cabernet. He didn't want to gush over a meal that appeared to be an ordinary, everyday occurrence at her house, even though it seemed to be a highlight for him this evening.

In the background, the kitchen radio played an Eagles song about taking it easy, and he decided it certainly fit the mood tonight.

"Guess what," Lisa said. "I scored two goals today, Mom. Coach Patricia says I'm her best kicker, and she wants me to try out for the traveling team when school starts."

Megan blessed her daughter with a smile, a spark of pride lighting her eyes. "I'm so proud of you, honey. You definitely are one of the best players. But why don't we just stick with the regular soccer league this year. You'll be busy with school, and I heard those travel teams take up a lot of time. They also cost quite a bit. Maybe when you're older, we can talk about it."

Clay figured Megan didn't like having to tell her children no. And he imagined it might be difficult for her to imply that things were tight financially, especially in front of an outsider, but she'd handled the situation well—even if Lisa's face had turned into a sullen pout that would rival any that Collette had ever thrown his way.

Hoping to distract the girl and turn the mood at the table back to a lighter one, Clay asked Lisa, "What other sports have you been playing at summer camp?"

"Basketball, tennis—which is *boooooring*—softball and everything. Flag football is my favorite, but Coach Patricia made me sit out of the game last time because I kept getting too many fouls for tackling."

Tyler took a break from shoving bread into his mouth long enough to say, "Football sucks. And it's not for girls anyway, Lisa."

"Is, too. Just 'cause you can't play as good as me doesn't mean it sucks."

Tyler clucked his tongue, then went back to eating.

"We have another game tomorrow afternoon at the park near Zorba's," Lisa said. "You want to watch me play football tomorrow, Mr. Johnson? If you come, I'll try my best not to tackle anyone."

Football, whether it was tackle or flag or whatever, had never been one of Clay's favorite sports. But how could he resist the cute little pixie with big brown eyes, loose braids and a freckled nose?

"Sure," he said. "Maybe I can close the shop early and walk over to the park." Clay speared another crispy roasted potato from his plate and popped it into his mouth.

"Well, I don't want to go to a stupid football game," Tyler said. "But if you and my mom want to both go, I could watch the shop for you."

Clay could certainly relate to the boy's desire to hide out at Zorba's rather than hang around a bunch of football players with their sports-fanatic parents yelling on the sidelines. "If your mom is okay with it, I don't mind."

"It's all right with me," Megan said, "but the shop stays locked up while you're there, Tyler. I don't want you dealing with any of the customers. And no messing around on the new shipment of laptops."

Lisa pumped her fist in the air, and Tyler promised to be on his best behavior.

"And stop feeding Pancho under the table," Megan added. "He has enough bad habits as it is."

Clay couldn't blame Lisa for passing food to the dog. The poor mutt had missed a lot of meals while he'd been on the run.

"Okay," Lisa said to her mom. "Then can I be excused? There's a special on ESPN about the best girls' college basketball teams."

What? No TV shows about a fairy or a princess or a bunch of pastel animals that could sing and dance?

Clay almost laughed at the thought of the little girl wanting to watch ESPN rather than the Disney Channel. But he supposed the precocious tomboy stood out in her class at school just as much as Tyler did. That made them both social outcasts—just as he'd once been.

"No way," Tyler countered. "Mom, you said I could watch that Bill Gates interview tonight. And I need to learn more about him because of that report I have to do for that dumb summer enrichment program you're making me attend."

Megan blew out a sigh. "I forgot about that. But either way, you can both record your shows. You're not going to watch anything until you wash the dishes and finish your other chores."

There was some grumbling, but the kids picked up their plates and headed into the kitchen, Pancho following behind them.

"Sorry about that," Megan said. "I wish I could tell you that they're not normally like this, but they're kids. And I have to admit that when it comes to dinnertime at my house, this is what you can expect to see most nights."

"Don't apologize. Lisa and Tyler are great kids with

unique personalities. They're also well-mannered. You're a good mom."

"Thanks. I try, but it's hard sometimes." She took a sip of her wine, as if she thought better about unloading her single-mom troubles on him. "So what were you like as a kid?"

"Well-mannered," Clay responded. "With a unique personality."

She smiled, and he leaned back into his chair. He didn't know if it was the wine or his full stomach, the down-to-earth setting or the lovely woman seated next to him, but he hadn't felt this warm and content in a long time.

Of course, that contentment waffled when the song coming from the kitchen radio switched to an old Rolling Stones hit, reminding him of his mother, who used to play the Stones when she was in one of her manic moods.

During those phases, she'd be flying over the top, but at least she'd been happy and smiling. It was when he'd come home to find her listening to Celine Dion that he knew she was coming down and heading into the spiral of depression.

"Seriously, though," she continued, "where did you grow up?"

"I was born in Houston, but we moved around a lot when I was a kid."

"Why is that? Were your parents in the military?"

"It was just me and my mom. And, well, she never really could hold down a job."

Clay didn't know why he was opening up like that with Megan. He hadn't told anyone other than his mentor, retired detective Hank Lazaro, about his childhood, although plenty of social workers had access to the information in his case file.

But for some reason, he didn't want to hold anything back. Well, other than his name and his occupation, which was big enough to be a whopper.

He'd clear that up in short order, though, and confess his reason for not being honest about his identity from day one. And while he knew her well enough to trust her with that information now, there was something else holding him back. Another reason to keep the truth under wraps for a while longer.

Megan seemed to be drawn to the real man inside him and not just to his money and fame, which was a first for him. So shouldn't he give it some time to see where it went?

"That must have been really hard on you," she said. "We moved just that one time when I was in high school, and it devastated me. I've always been one of those home-and-hearth kind of girls."

As Mick Jagger sang on, the kindness in Megan's big brown eyes encouraged him to continue.

Aw, what the hell. If he couldn't be completely forthcoming about his name and true occupation, at least he could be honest about everything else.

"My mother wasn't like the other moms, but I didn't know why until I got older. She had bipolar disorder. I understand her illness now, but even though I knew she was sick and that she couldn't help being the way she was, that didn't make it easy for a scrawny and nerdy kid like me."

"*You?* Scrawny and nerdy? That's hard to believe."

"Oh, you can believe it. In fact, when I first met Tyler, he reminded me a lot of myself at that age." Clay tossed her a grin and a wink. "But he has a beautiful mom who looks out for him, even if he doesn't always realize how lucky he is."

Megan smiled at his attempt to change the subject and to compliment her, but tears welled in her eyes, threatening to overflow.

He didn't like thinking that he'd had anything to do with putting them there. Nor did he want her pity. He was about to tell her so when she said, "That makes me angry."

Whoa. Pity he'd expected, but not anger.

"I hate it that the other kids picked on you for being different. It's so unfair. What about your dad? Did you ever see him? Didn't he help you out?"

"Nope, he was her college professor. And he dumped her as soon as he learned she was pregnant."

"He was her teacher? That was unethical of him to get involved with a student. I'd think she could have caused him some real trouble."

"She loved him. Besides, she was too unstable to follow through on any charges. In fact, she had her first breakdown right after I was born. After she picked up the pieces, we moved to the next town. But things just repeated in the same cycle like that until I was a junior in high school. It was all I ever knew."

"So what happened then? Did she get better?"

"She finally landed a job working nights at a medical lab. It was always easier for her when she didn't have to interact with too many people, but it left me alone a lot. Anyway, one evening, before she went to work, she told me that she loved me and that she wished she could have been a better mother. She was always saying things like that when she was in her low moods, but for some reason, it struck me as odd that night. It was like she wanted to ingrain those words in my mind."

And it had worked. Clay glanced out the kitchen window, saw the sun had gone down. And while he'd have preferred to shake the last memory he had of his mother, he figured he'd already come this far, already revealed so much.

He returned his gaze to Megan, who was watching him intently—not pressuring him to speak, as some of the social workers had, but just waiting for him to decide when and how much to share.

"The cops woke me up around midnight and told me that my mom had been in a single-car accident. The vehicle was found slammed into a tree. No skid marks from braking or swerving. It was never ruled a suicide, but deep down I knew."

Megan shook her head, wiping a tear from her cheek. "I'm so sorry. I can't imagine how horrible that must have been for you. I lost my dad when I was a freshman in high school, and it was really hard. But he died of natural causes—a heart attack."

Silence stretched between them, buffered by something else. Sympathy maybe. Understanding? Friendship?

Clay wasn't sure what it was, but sharing his dark and dreary past with Megan seemed like the right thing to do.

"Since I was still underage," he added, "the state stepped in. I went to a foster home, but it wasn't too bad. I kept to myself, finished high school and stayed out of trouble—for the most part, anyway. And I ended up… Well, I did okay."

"You mentioned not meeting your dad until you were an adult," she said. "Do you ever see him?"

"I'd just started Zorba the Geek— I mean I had just started *working* there." Oops. That was a close one. "I'd gone through some of my mom's old papers to find out his name and where he lived. Then I did an internet search and learned that he'd changed teaching positions and moved around to several different universities over the years. I figured my mom was so hurt she'd written him off and had never kept in contact with him."

"Is that what happened?"

"I'd always thought or rather hoped that he'd wanted to know me and have a relationship but that we'd moved around so much that he had no idea how to find me. But no, that's not what happened."

Megan poured more wine into his glass as if knowing that his revelation wasn't an easy one to make. But then again, she'd had children with a deadbeat who didn't want the responsibility of being a father, so she probably suspected how a surprise meeting with a man and his unwanted child had gone.

"At first he said he didn't remember my mom. He denied that she'd ever been his student. He claimed to be a renowned scholar and researcher who'd never cheated on his wife in the thirty years they'd been married. And he also said that he'd never do anything unprofessional, like dating a student, especially one who was a 'schizo.' Then he closed the door in my face."

Megan reached across the table and placed her hand over his in a move that was both comforting and heart stirring at the same time.

It was nice, yet it was weird, too. Here he was, telling Megan something he'd never told anyone, sharing feelings he'd kept hidden for years and being far more honest with her than he'd ever been with people who actually knew his real name.

"I'm sorry," she said.

"About him turning out to be a jerk?" Clay shrugged. "He might have denied it, but he told me a lot that day. My mom had been diagnosed as bipolar and not schizophrenic, but I'd never mentioned her mental health issues to him. So when he called her a schizo, it was obvious that he knew exactly who she was, and that he was trying to cover his ass."

They continued to sit like that, hands clasped—as if they'd been bonded in some unexpected way.

"You know," Megan finally said, "people always tell me that my kids are better off without their father, that it's good my ex took a hike. They say that having no dad is better than having some self-absorbed, washed-up, football-playing has-been in their lives. And maybe that's true. Maybe it was better that you never had to deal with Professor Jerkface. But that doesn't make a father's abandonment hurt any less."

She hit the nail on the head, because that was exactly how Clay had felt. "It would have been one thing if I'd chosen to shut *him* out of *my* life. But when he closed the door in my face, the rejection hurt."

"It was his loss, too. You really overcame a lot and made the most out of your life."

Megan had no idea how far he'd come, but his dad did. Clay never liked boasting about his personal success, and with Megan not really knowing who he was, he couldn't very well do it now. But he'd gotten the upper hand and he could give her an abbreviated version of the rest of the story.

"A few years ago, my father found out all that I'd... Well, when he heard that I worked for Geekon Enterprises and thought I might have some pull within the company, he tried to establish a relationship with me. But what he really wanted was financial backing for a new research project."

"Did you help him?"

"I did my homework first. And through some personal contacts and a thorough internet search, I learned that he'd been fired from several teaching positions due to inappropriate contact with undergrads. And because he hadn't done any relevant research in his field, he was becoming a laughingstock in the academic world."

"I hope you closed the door right in his face, the way he did to you."

Clay smiled at the feisty redhead, making a mental note to always stay on her good side. "I would have if he'd have even had the decency to come see me in person. Unfortunately, I had to settle for hanging up on him and telling Zoe to block all his calls."

"That was a smart move." Clay didn't tell her that he'd authorized Geekon Enterprises to fund several similar research projects at competing universities, knowing that other professors getting national acclaim for discoveries his father wanted to make would be the nail in the man's career coffin.

At that point, Tyler returned to the dining room carrying a tray of cupcakes. "We finished in the kitchen. And Lisa said I could have her dessert if she can watch her dumb girls'-basketball show first. So I'm going to take Pancho outside to play a little bit." Then he snagged two of the small frosted cakes and sprinted out the door, Pancho fast on his heels.

Thank goodness for the interruption. If Clay wasn't careful, he'd be dumping even more on Megan, hoping for more of those doe-eyed gazes or those sympathetic touches.

And if truth be told, he'd much rather be lying on the floor with her, tangled up in computer cords and wondering how to hide his ever-growing arousal.

He was also going to have to hide his raw and ragged emotions from her, too. She had a way of stirring up the feelings he'd successfully tamped down years ago. And he could really use a little break from her sympathetic gaze, as well as her gentle touch.

"Do you mind if I talk to Tyler now?" he asked.

"No, not at all. Please do."

Clay got to his feet and headed for the sliding door Tyler and the dog had just used, determined to put some distance between him and Megan before he began to believe his name really was Peyton Johnson.

Megan had never met a man as open and as honest as Peyton. Just talking to him this evening, when he'd laid his heart open, had touched something deep inside of her. It was enough to make her rethink her decision about not getting involved with another man until her kids were older and had moved out on their own.

But how could she consider lowering her guard around him when she knew he'd be leaving soon?

And why was she even fantasizing about a relationship with him when he hadn't made any move in that direction? Well, other than a few heated glances and that tumble to the floor earlier today.

Peyton hadn't mentioned where he lived, although she suspected it might be Houston, since that was the office that had sent him to Brighton Valley. He'd also mentioned having Zoe block his calls from his father.

Did that mean his job at the corporate office was so important that he had his own personal secretary? Or did Zoe assist several different employees in that capacity?

Either way, it sounded as though Peyton was pretty much entrenched with the Houston office. So what were the chances of him moving to Brighton Valley?

Slim to none, she'd bet.

Still, she couldn't help wondering what her life might be like if she and Peyton were to strike up a romantic relationship.

Of course, if he wasn't going to settle in town permanently, that wasn't going to do her any good. So she'd better stop wasting her time thinking about it.

Instead she'd focus on how happy she was that he'd taken an interest in Tyler. The poor kid could sure use a male influence in his life, especially since he'd never bonded with his father.

At first she'd assumed Todd wasn't comfortable with newborns. And then she'd blamed it on him being too busy with his studies and playing college football. And when a career in the NFL never panned out and he had to get a regular job, she'd chalked it up to the two of them having no common interests. But Todd hadn't bonded with Lisa, either.

The truth was, Todd Redding hadn't cared about anyone but himself. And trying to create a family and a home with him had been an impossible dream from the get-go.

When the sliding door eased open and Peyton returned to the dining room, their eyes met, and her pulse rate slipped into overdrive. For a moment, a world of romantic possibilities opened up, but she decided not to pin her heart on any of them.

"How'd it go?" she asked.

"Okay. I asked him about that slight bruise and the small scratch I'd seen on his face earlier. He said it happened while he was chasing the dog. But on the outside chance someone's still teasing him, I showed him some defensive moves, like my buddy once taught me. I think it'll give him a little confidence."

"Thank you, Peyton. You have no idea how much I appreciate your help."

Before either of them could comment further, Tyler entered the house, the dog tagging along behind him. "I have a question for you. Since you work for Geekon and Zorba's, I was wondering if you knew Clay Jenkins."

Peyton stiffened, and Megan wondered why. Did it bother him to be reminded of the home office and that his days in Brighton Valley were coming to an end? She hoped so, because it was bothering her more than she cared to admit.

"Why do you want to know about him?" Peyton narrowed his gaze, then rubbed his chin, much the way her grandpa used to stroke his beard when he pondered a perplexing question.

"Because I have to do a report on a hero of mine, and I was going to do it on Bill Gates or Steve Jobs or someone like that. But I was thinking that maybe I should write about Clay Jenkins since he's the guy my mom works for. And since you might even know him personally."

"I…uh, know who he is," Peyton said.

"What's he like?"

Peyton's stance eased, and his lips quirked into a slow grin. "Clay's a lot like you—not always respected by his peers, but he's much brighter than they are. He's also loyal to his friends and determined to succeed. But I think you'd be better off doing that report on Bill Gates, especially since you're taping that special about him on TV tonight."

"Yeah, maybe you're right."

As Tyler left the room, Peyton turned to Megan and crossed his arms. Then he averted his gaze and scanned the dining room.

"You have a nice house," he said. "It's homey. And a great place to raise kids."

"Thanks. This was my grandparents' house, so I spent a lot of time here when I was growing up. I learned to cook, bake, can fruit and make jam here. And after my grandparents died, they left the house to my mom. She and my stepdad are traveling, so I'm house-sitting."

"You don't actually live here?" he asked.

Moving home after her divorce had been a necessity and not something she was eager to admit. But since Todd hadn't fulfilled his obligation to pay child support, and she'd refused to go to his wealthy family and ask for their assistance, she'd had no other choice.

"Yes, we live here. And until my mom and stepdad get back, which probably won't be until Christmas or early next year, we have the house to ourselves."

"Well, you're doing a fine job of keeping the home fires burning. A guy could find himself getting way too cozy here." He smiled, then glanced at his wristwatch. "It's getting late, so I'd better head back to the apartment. Thanks so much for having me over for dinner.

It was the best meal I've had in ages. In fact, I can't remember when I've had better."

"You're welcome to join us anytime." Gosh, had she just issued an open invitation? Not that she wanted to renege on it, but what in the world was she going to do if Peyton started coming to dinner every night?

But more important, what was she going to do when he left town for good?

She'd been so distrustful of him when he'd first arrived, but he was proving to be a good friend. She was also moved by his openness and honesty. How refreshing it was to meet a man she could trust.

As Peyton opened the door, she followed him outside. The moon was especially bright, and a light summer breeze stirred the fragrance of the orchard at night.

It also stirred the scent of his cologne, which mingled with the sparks that zinged between them whenever they were alone.

"Thanks for everything," she said, not going into detail but hoping he knew what was in her heart.

Peyton placed a hand along her jaw, sending a ripple of heat clean through her. As his gaze locked on to hers, his thumb caressed her cheek. "I have no business doing this."

"Doing what?" she asked, the words coming out in a wispy, choppy breath. But she sensed what he meant, what he was about to do—and she welcomed it. As his lips lowered to hers, she closed her eyes and let her romantic dreams take flight.

Chapter Nine

As their lips met, Megan slipped her arms around Peyton's neck, kissing him slowly at first, as if they were teenagers testing the waters of sexual attraction. But the shyness didn't last long.

The moment their tongues met, she leaned into him, losing herself in his arms, in his taste. And within a couple of heartbeats, the kiss exploded with passion.

Maybe it was the fact that she'd been celibate for so long. Or maybe it was because Peyton was such an amazing kisser who promised to be an even better lover.

At this point, the only thing that really mattered was that she wanted more from Peyton than she'd ever imagined she would. And she didn't want this kiss to ever end.

She had no idea how long they stood outside, wrapped in each other's arms, breaths mingling, hands caressing, exploring. It seemed that she was caught up in something much bigger, much stronger than she'd anticipated. But she finally drew her mouth from his just so she could take a breath. Yet she continued to hold him tightly, to rest her cheek against his.

"I…uh…" Peyton blew out a ragged breath. "Well, if I'd known how nice your good-night kiss was going to be, I would have told you I had to leave sooner than this."

She smiled. "I didn't expect it to be so nice, either."

"Neither did I, but I'm glad it happened."

So was she. Now all she had to do was figure out what sharing a knee-weakening, breath-stealing heated kiss like that meant—and what she wanted to do about it.

She'd known that she was sexually attracted to him. But she'd never guessed that they would have the kind of chemistry that would set the night on fire.

"I guess this complicates things," she said.

"Just a bit."

She blew out a sigh, then pulled free of his embrace. "I guess we should call it a day and see how we feel about things in the morning."

"Maybe so."

Yet neither of them took a step in either direction. That is, until Lisa swung open the door and popped her head outside. "Oh, good. You didn't leave yet, Mr. Johnson. I wanted to remind you about my game tomorrow. Since my mom doesn't work on Wednesdays, she can't remind you about it. And I don't want you to forget."

Peyton reached over and gave one of her braids a gentle tug. "I won't forget. What time does it start?"

"Three o'clock."

"All right. I'll see you there."

When Lisa shut the door, leaving them alone again, Peyton said, "I suppose that means I won't be getting any breakfast burritos or warm muffins to eat with my coffee tomorrow. I'd forgotten that it was Wednesday."

So had Megan, but that wasn't a bad thing. It actually meant that they'd have more time to let things sink in.

She feared she might be falling for Peyton—as uneasy as that thought made her. And she was going to need more than a few hours to wrap her mind around that possibility.

And to decide just what in the heck she was going to do about it.

As Wednesday wore on, Clay found himself wandering around the shop, unable to get much work done. He'd been so caught up in that amazing but unexpected goodbye kiss he'd shared with Megan last night that he couldn't seem to focus on anything else.

It might have started out as a sweet and friendly way to say *I'll see you later,* but that wasn't the way it had ended up. Instead it promised that they'd be seeing a hell of a lot more of each other. And that they'd be sharing a few good-morning kisses, too.

Damn. What was he going to do about that woman? He wasn't about to settle in Brighton Valley, but was he ready for the alternative? Did he want to tell her who he was, then ride off with her and the kids in the sunset?

He raked his hand through his hair for the umpteenth time, then clucked his tongue. He wasn't so sure he wanted to leave town without her.

She'd said that they would have to wait and see how they felt about things in the morning, but he sure hoped she didn't ask him what conclusion he'd come up with, because he was still just as befuddled now as he'd been last night.

Befuddled? Hell, it was more like bewitched.

Somehow he'd managed to make it through the day. Then, at a quarter to three, he placed a closed sign on the front door, locked up the shop and made the walk to the park, where he'd promised to meet up with Megan and the kids.

It was a fairly short walk down Main Street to the town square, then another block to the park. He'd no more than stepped onto the walkway that led to the ball field, when he spotted a familiar face—Rick Martinez.

Clay had been meaning to call his old friend, but he hadn't done so yet. A while back, Rick had asked him to help him locate Joey, his younger brother, who'd left town ten years ago and had never been heard of since.

Rick had hired a P.I., who hadn't had any luck. And so he'd thought Clay might have better luck using his computer skills.

It wouldn't be the first time Clay had helped the guy who'd stepped in and stopped Todd Redding's harassment back when they'd both been at Washington High in Wexler.

After Rick had transferred to Brighton Valley High and mentioned his interest in Mallory Dickinson, a beautiful blond honor student, Clay had hacked into the BVHS computer system and found her phone number and address, along with a few other pertinent details. He'd passed it to Rick—a gift from one friend to another.

Several weeks later, Rick and Mallory started dating. Clay had been happy for his friend, although he'd felt like an outsider again. Then, when Mallory left town, and the couple had eventually broken up, Rick had been devastated. It had been enough to make a guy leery of falling in love—that is, if Clay ever found the right girl.

And now he wondered if Megan might be that girl....

"Well, look what the proverbial cat dragged in." Rick, who'd been heading for the drinking fountain, stopped in his tracks, then extended his hand in greeting. "How long have you been in town?"

"A little more than a week. I called you a few days after I arrived, but your receptionist said you and your family were vacationing in Hawaii."

"We just got back. I have an associate working with me at the clinic now, so I can finally take some time off."

"I'm glad to hear it. How are Mallory and Lucas doing?"

"They're both great." Rick cocked his head. "But look at you, Clay. I never thought I'd see the day when you would cut your long hair, shave that beard or toss your glasses. What's that all about? Going for a new style?"

"Actually, I've been trying to lay low. No one down at the store knows who I really am. In fact, I told them my name is Peyton Johnson and that I'm an accountant who was sent by corporate to help them convert to a new system."

"When you mentioned coming to Brighton Valley to check things out at the store, I had no idea you were going to go undercover."

"Yeah, well, it seemed like a good idea at the time, but now I'm going to have to figure out a way to come clean. I'm just not ready to do that yet."

"Why? Do you still think there's something under-handed going on at the store?"

"No, not anymore." Clay told Rick about Megan, about how things were warming up between them—and how nice it was to know a woman liked him for something other than the things he could buy her or the places he could take her.

"Megan's a nice woman. She also makes great muffins, jams and jellies. We make a point of stopping by her booth at the farmers market."

"Yes, I know. But if our paths cross, especially if I'm with her and the kids, pretend that we've never met until now."

"I won't say anything—or call you by name. But I can't lie for you, especially to my wife. And to make matters even more difficult, she and Megan are friends."

"I understand. And for the record, I don't intend to keep it a secret much longer. I'll be coming clean soon."

"Good," Rick said. "That'll make things easier, at least for me."

"I should have realized Mallory and Megan would be friends. They both went to Brighton Valley High."

"Actually, they never ran in the same crowds when they were in school. Megan was a cheerleader, and Mallory hung out with the honor students—that is, until she met me."

Clay remembered those days in high school, when Rick had been aimless and prone to getting into trouble. "But at least things finally worked out for you guys."

"It took a ten-year separation, but yeah. Things worked out great. And I'll let you in on a secret. We're going to have a baby at the end of December."

"Just in time for Christmas?"

"Maybe. Or New Year's. Either way, we couldn't be happier." Rick's smile faded a bit. "Well, the only thing that would make it better would be to find my brother. Have you had any luck?"

"Actually, I finally got a lead about two weeks ago, although it isn't much of one yet. So I hate to get your hopes up until I hear back from a guy."

"When Joey left town, he disappeared off the face of the earth. So your lead is the first one I've had. What did you turn up?"

"I found a retired marine who took the same bus Joey did when he ran off. And he might know something."

"You haven't talked to him yet?"

"The guy lives in some remote fishing village in Mexico. He has to go into a nearby town just to get cell-phone service or an internet connection, and even then it's sketchy at best. But I sent him an email, and I'm waiting to hear back. So I'll keep you posted."

"Great. Thanks."

Before either man could comment further, Tyler walked toward them with Pancho on a leash. "Can I get the key to the repair shop, Mr. Johnson?"

"Sure." Clay reached into his pocket and handed it over to the boy.

"That's a nice dog," Rick said. "But he's way too thin."

Tyler patted the top of the dog's head. "Yeah, I know. But you should have seen him before we gave him a bath and fed him, Dr. Martinez."

"Pancho was a stray," Peyton explained. "The kids found him yesterday."

Rick stooped to give Pancho a scratch behind his

ear. "Tell your mom to bring him in for a free exam—
and for his shots."

"Cool. Thanks, Doctor. I'll do that."

When Tyler took off toward the repair shop on Main,
Clay said, "I'll pay for the dog's exam and his shots.
You don't need to offer them a freebie."

"I'm not going to charge either one of you. I run an
animal rescue, and Pancho probably would have ended
up at my place if Megan's kids hadn't found him first.
So I would have fattened him up and made sure he was
healthy before finding him a home. I've always been a
sucker for strays."

That was true. And Clay was lucky Rick had seen
him as a stray who needed rescuing all those years ago.

Assuming a stray wandered through life looking for
a place where he really fit in, then in some ways, Clay
supposed he still was one.

The next afternoon while Megan went to pick up
her kids from school, Clay sat in front of the computer, checking email. When he spotted one from Dia-
blo Perro, the retired marine he'd been trying to reach,
he clicked the mouse, and the message opened right up.

Yep, you found the right Mack McGinnis. And as a matter of fact, me and a couple of buddies did take the
Old Gray Dog from Texas to California about ten years
back. That's one trip I'll never forget. It was raining
like hell. The bus broke down a couple of times. There
was a pileup on the interstate near Tucson. Turned out
okay, but I thought we'd never make it to Camp Pend-
leton in time and would end up in the brig. So a few

of us caught a ride with a family heading to the coast. Why do you ask?

Clay had waited two weeks for this response, so there was no telling how long he'd have to wait for the next one. But he had a lead, and he wasn't about to let it go. So he typed in the reason for his query.

I'm looking for a kid named Joey Martinez. He was on that same bus but was never accounted for in Tucson or in San Diego. He was seventeen and had been a foster kid. His brother lost touch with him and wants to find him. By any chance do you remember seeing him or know where he might have gone?

"What are you doing?" Tyler asked as he entered the back office.

Clay, who'd just clicked Send, said, "Not much. A friend of mine had asked me to look for his brother, a guy who went missing years ago. He hadn't been able to find him, and he thought I could do it through the internet."

"Did you?" Tyler asked. "Find him, I mean."

"Not yet, but I might have uncovered someone who ran into him."

"Wow. That's cool."

"It would be super cool if I actually found him and helped the two brothers reconnect."

Tyler bit down on his bottom lip. "Think you could help me do that?"

"Do what? Find someone?"

"Yeah. My dad. He and my mom split up, and I haven't seen him since. I don't expect them to get married again or anything like that. He ended up with someone else. But he doesn't write or call or send money or anything. And…well, it's just that…" Tyler bit down on his bottom lip again, then looked back at Clay. "He divorced my mom, but don't you think he'd want to have a relationship with his son?"

Clay, more than anyone, understood a kid's desire to think that a dad or a mom or some absent person in his life adored him and was just waiting to be found. But when he'd gone in search of his own father, he'd felt worse after finding him than if he hadn't looked for him at all.

Clay wanted to spare Tyler from going through the same heartbreaking experience, especially since he'd gathered that Megan's ex-husband wasn't any nobler than Professor Bradley Madigan had turned out to be.

And even if things didn't turn out the same way for Tyler, and his dad did end up wanting to be a part of his kids' lives, Clay wasn't so sure he liked the idea of the guy waltzing back into the picture like some long-lost hero when he'd been anything but.

"I can't help you with that, Tyler. Sometimes men who are weak and irresponsible disappear for good reasons. And finding them only stirs up trouble for the people who've moved on with their lives. My advice is to just let it be."

Tyler glanced down and studied his scuffed sneakers for a moment, then looked up and gave a little shrug. "Okay, I'll think about it."

When the boy walked away, Clay went back to work. It didn't take long before he lost himself in it, just the way he always used to.

It was kind of funny, but as eager as he'd been to slip

in and out of Brighton Valley, he was finding that he'd actually missed the hands-on work. And that he didn't mind small town life the way he'd thought he might. In fact, he liked the people he'd met.

Maybe he ought to tell Megan that the corporate office had asked him to stick around long enough to help Don ease back into a full-time position.

But was that really the wisest thing for him to do? How involved did he want to get with Megan and her kids?

After that heated kiss they'd shared the other night, he was torn between hightailing it out of here and waiting to see where another kiss might lead.

He'd barely signed off his email account, when Megan entered the back office, bringing another woman with her. Because the older woman wore a long flowing scarf on her head, the kind chemo patients wore to cover their hair loss, he suspected that she was Don's wife.

"Peyton," Megan said, "this is Cindy Carpenter."

Clay got to his feet and greeted the woman with a handshake. "It's nice to finally meet you. How's Don doing?"

"He's recovering nicely—thanks to you and to everyone in the Houston office. The company has been so good to us that we have no other choice but to get better."

"I'm glad to hear that," Peyton said.

"So while I was in town, I thought I should stop by and thank you for staying to help Megan in the shop."

"I'm glad it worked out." Peyton looked at Megan, who tossed him a warm smile.

"Cindy was just telling me about all the things that Geekon Enterprises has done for them," Megan said.

"And I'm amazed. I guess not all big companies are so focused on the bottom line that they forget about the people who work for them."

Clay returned her smile, although the fact was, Geekon Enterprises hadn't been any different from what she'd expected until he'd stepped into his undercover role in Brighton Valley. And while he was still making changes in the HR departments in all the subsidiaries, like improving the health insurance and creating a sunshine fund, that wasn't the way things were just a month ago.

"Well, I'd better go," Cindy said. "I just came into town to pick up some groceries. And I have to get my frozen food home before it melts."

"I'll walk you out to the car," Megan told her.

"Tyler and Lisa," Cindy said, "come outside with us. I just happen to have some ice-cream bars you two can have."

With that, both kids followed the women out the back of the shop, leaving Clay alone. But he didn't have a chance to return to his seat before the bell on the front door jangled again.

"Is anyone here?" Rick Martinez called out.

"I am." Clay left his work on the desk to meet his friend.

Rick placed a bag on the counter. "I brought some special dog food for Pancho. It's what I feed all my rescue dogs. It's loaded with nutrients."

"Thanks. I'm sure Megan and the kids will appreciate it."

Rick scanned the shop. "Where is everyone?"

"They're walking Cindy Carpenter out to her car."

"Have you had a chance to tell Megan who you are yet?" Rick asked, lowering his voice.

"Not yet, but I'm going to. I just have to figure out how and when to do it."

"I don't understand. What are you waiting for?"

Clay wasn't sure. How long did he want to continue living a fantasy? He couldn't stay in Brighton Valley forever.

"Oh," Rick said. "I get it."

"Get what?"

"You're feeling guilty about all the BS you've been spinning."

"Well, it didn't start out as BS. But yeah, you're right. I don't want her to see me in a bad light."

"There's only one reason for you to feel guilty and to drag your feet. You're falling for her."

Clay wanted to argue, but Rick had a point. And a strong one. "Even if you were right, I wouldn't know how to tell her that the guy she thinks she knows and cares about doesn't exist."

"Doesn't he?"

Clay clucked his tongue. "I'm not sure what's real and what isn't. So how can I expect her to see it all clearly? Besides, I've never been good when it comes to dealing with people."

"That's not true any longer. Look at you. You've built a multimillion-dollar company—or is it billions now?—from scratch. And I've seen pictures of some of the women you've had on your arm at those fancy functions you go to all the time…like that model. What was her name?"

"Collette. And it took me months to finally get it through her head that I didn't want to see her anymore.

In fact, I just ended things once and for all a week ago—
and that was through a text message because my face-
to-face conversations and phone calls with her weren't
working."

"You're making this more complicated than it needs
to be."

Was he? Or was he just wanting to stretch the fantasy out as long as he could?

Was he actually waiting for Megan to fall for Peyton so he could spring some kind of Cinderella surprise on her?

As strange as it sounded, he wasn't sure if he could
seal the deal in his Peyton persona. Maybe it was time
to let her know he was Clay—and all he could offer
her and the kids.

Who wouldn't want to move away from Brighton
Valley? He could provide them with a home in the city.
Her financial worries would be over.

"I'll tell her the truth within the next couple of days,
but I have to make sure everything is right when I do."

"How are you going to do that?"

"Leave that to me." And to Zoe.

The wheels were beginning to turn, but Clay had a
plan, and it was bound to work. He'd take Megan on
a fairy-tale date in Houston—at a five-star restaurant.
Because of the two-hour drive, he'd get them a room—
or two, if she'd be more comfortable—for the night.

Maybe then she'd be impressed—and willing to forgive his lie.

Chapter Ten

Candlelight flickered on the linen-draped table, while several of the waitstaff stood to the side, hands behind them, ready to be of service. Yet Megan only had eyes for the handsome man who'd invited her out to dinner at one of the most elegant restaurants in Houston.

She'd been surprised when Peyton had invited her, and she had initially told him no. After all, who took a first date all the way to Houston on a Friday night?

And what woman who'd sworn off men since she and her husband had separated agreed to go on her very first date as a single woman knowing it would be an overnighter—albeit one that would be perfectly respectful?

But Peyton had been so sweet when he'd asked her, so thoughtful when he'd offered to get two separate rooms at a swanky hotel because of the distance they'd have to travel. Besides, when he'd said that she deserved to be wined and dined, well…she'd been flattered, to say the least. And in spite of the fact that she'd worried about how he could afford such an amazing evening, she'd agreed.

Caroline was thrilled that her single young friend was finally going out on a date and offered to keep the kids overnight.

So Megan and Peyton had locked up the shop early, and after leaving her car parked in the alley, they'd driven to downtown Houston. Once they'd checked into their adjoining rooms, they'd gotten dressed there.

Megan had been nervous but excited, too. And so far she was glad that she'd come. She'd never been treated like a princess before—and had never had a man be so attentive.

This night, with this man, was the kind of date a woman dreamed about.

After Peyton ordered a bottle of expensive California red wine, Megan asked, "Have you been to this restaurant often?"

"A few times, when I've come to the Houston office."

"Oh?" She leaned back in her seat. "You don't live and work here? I'd assumed you did."

Peyton took a drink of his water—the sparkling kind the waiter poured from a fancy bottle. "I visit all the district offices."

Megan had known he was good at his job. And that he wasn't a country bumpkin like her. But she hadn't realized his position with Zorba's had required him to travel so much. Apparently he was used to big cities and the finer things in life. He probably even had a corporate credit card.

Would he pay for their meal with it? Would he consider their date to be a business expense the company could write off? The thought that he might was a little unsettling, but she shrugged it off. He was an accountant. Surely he knew better than that.

The sommelier returned to their table and poured a small amount of wine in Peyton's glass, waiting for him to give his approval.

Did he consider this a business dinner? Was he taking pity on a poor single mother by showing her a good time?

She scolded herself for worrying about it. Instead she would just enjoy herself since she doubted that she'd ever experience another like this again.

So she took a sip of her wine, felt it warm her throat as she swallowed, then leaned back in her seat and gave her head a little shake to toss the hair from her face.

She'd worn it long tonight, and while she supposed it fit the occasion, she wasn't used to the strands tumbling loose along her shoulders. She'd also used more makeup than usual so she wouldn't be mistaken for a bright-eyed farm girl on her first trip to the big city.

Yet the cover-model hair, mascara and lip gloss made her feel a bit bolder. So did the formfitting black dress she'd found in the back of her closet.

She'd purchased the outfit several years ago when she'd realized her marriage was on the rocks. It had been her idea of a Hail Mary pass to try and save a dying relationship. But she'd never had the chance to wear the dress or the skimpy black bra and matching panties she'd bought that day. She'd no more than returned from her shopping spree when she'd learned that Todd had been cheating.

"So," she said to the handsome man sitting across

from her, "if you bounce around to all the offices, where do you call home?"

"I have a condo in Silicon Valley, but I've never really put down roots anywhere."

How sad. She reached across the table and placed her hand over his. She'd meant it to be a sympathetic gesture, but either the wine or the sexy ensemble she'd torn the tags off while in the hotel room just an hour earlier had given her the courage to caress his knuckles. "Don't you ever get tired of traveling from one place to another?"

"Moving around is all I've ever known. I'm used to it." He turned his palm up and took her hand in his, holding her captive. His thumb traced lazy circles along her wrist, the sizzling strokes sending sparks of heat to her core.

She had the sudden urge to ask if he ever planned to settle down, but a loaded question like that would kill the mood faster than if she dumped a glass of ice water on his head.

All she needed was for him to think she wanted to be the woman he'd choose to settle down with.

And when she thought about it, did it really matter what he planned to do? She finally had her life just the way she wanted it. And she certainly wasn't ready to let another man come into it and shake things up.

But in the flickering candlelight, as the attraction sparked over their table, she realized this wasn't just a business dinner. Nor was it Peyton's way of showing a country girl a nice time.

This was definitely his idea of a date. And while she knew a permanent relationship between the two of them could never be, what would it hurt to live in the here and now—just for one amazing night?

When the waiter came to take their orders, they continued to hold hands as she shared stories of her childhood and they both told little anecdotes that seemed so far removed from the people they were today. They laughed and teased and drank more wine than she was used to.

She fed him a bite of her balsamic-glazed filet medallions, and he insisted she try his duck confit.

Over the next hour, they weren't coworkers or merely friends. They were... Well, they weren't lovers. At least, not yet. But there was definitely something going on. And judging by the way Peyton's gaze caressed her and the way she tingled inside when he did, she knew the feeling was mutual.

After a decadent dessert of crème brûlée with fresh raspberries, Megan decided that this had been one of the most enjoyable evenings of her life. She didn't know if Peyton had intended it to be this romantic, but that didn't diminish the fact that she'd never been wined and dined—and she liked it.

In high school Todd had taken her to the Tastee Cone on their first date. And when he was in college, they usually went to sports bars with his buddies.

A romantic evening consisted of him bringing home chicken wings and pizza so she wouldn't have to cook. And then he'd grab a beer and kick off his smelly sneakers before turning on *SportsCenter*. Was it any wonder tonight was so magical?

She knew she shouldn't get her hopes up that Peyton would stick around Brighton Valley—or that anything more could ever become of their date tonight—but she couldn't help it. There was something very nice about him, something wholesome and appealing. Something kind and trustworthy.

After Peyton paid the bill with a credit card—she had no idea which one he'd used, and she no longer cared—he pulled out her chair, and she stood. Then he placed his hand on her lower back and they made their way to the front of the restaurant.

The maître d' smiled at Peyton as they exited. "It was a pleasure serving you, Mr. Jenkins."

In the dimly lit entryway, Megan spotted a flush on Peyton's face, although he didn't correct the man.

You'd think that after dropping that much money in the restaurant, the staff would pay enough attention to the credit-card receipt and call a customer by his correct name.

Megan slipped her arm around Peyton's waist and tried to appease his ego. "Johnson is a common name. I'm sure with all the customers coming in and out in such a big city it's easy for them to get confused."

He looked at her, a furrow deep between his brows; then a smile spread across his face. "You're right. It just took me by surprise." Then he slipped his own arm around her, as well, and they began the short walk back to the hotel.

"Dinner was wonderful," she said as they passed couples dressed to the nines and a few university students clustered together outside an upscale bar.

"I thought so, too."

Just ahead, pushing a grocery cart loaded with all his worldly possessions, a scruffy man with a shaggy beard approached.

"Hey, buddy," he said to Peyton. "You got an extra cigarette I could have?"

The man wore a dirty army jacket and held a brown paper–covered bottle. "No, I don't smoke," Peyton said. "Besides, those things will kill you."

Megan suspected the poor man's liver would probably kill him before the tobacco would, but she still felt sorry for him.

She'd always tried to help the homeless, although Todd used to scold her for it. He claimed she was enabling people who ought to go out and get a real job and stop being a drain on society. That pithy observation, of course, had come from a guy whose family had always supplemented his income and enabled him right and left.

But she no longer had to listen to Todd, so she reached into her small clutch. Peyton stopped her. She assumed he was going to tell her the same thing Todd had. Instead he pulled a money clip loaded with bills from his pocket.

She'd watched him remove his wallet on occasion, but she'd never seen him with a wad of cash like the one he carried tonight. Was he crazy? He was going to get mugged on the street if he wasn't careful.

Peyton peeled out a couple of bills from the inside of the fold, then gave them to the man.

"God bless you, sir." The homeless man reached out his dirty, weathered hand, and in a move that surprised her, Peyton took it. Those long, smooth fingers looked unnaturally clean against the dark, dirt-encrusted fingernails that gripped them with appreciation.

As the man pushed his cart down the street, Megan

said, "That was one of the most generous and sweetest things I've ever seen."

"I wouldn't call it generous." Peyton gave the man one last glance, then slipped his hand along her waist.

"Um, I hope you don't think I'm snobbish, but would you mind if I asked you if you wanted to use some hand sanitizer?" She opened her small clutch and pulled out the tiny travel-size bottle of liquid antibacterial gel she always carried.

He laughed and squirted a large dollop in his palm before rubbing it in. "You're definitely not a snob. I've met my share of them. You are, however, a natural born mom."

She was glad to hear that, but she really hadn't wanted him to categorize her as a mother—especially tonight, when she wanted him to see her as a sexy and sophisticated woman.

The kind of woman who'd gone to Houston with a man who'd paid for them to have two adjoining hotel rooms—and who planned to suggest that they only use one.

Clay knew he shouldn't compare Megan, a small-town girl and single mom, to Collette or to any of the models or actresses he'd gone out with in the past. But by the time they'd been served their main courses, he'd realized that she was far more appealing than all his other dates combined.

Actually, he'd realized that in the past few weeks they'd been working together. But seeing Megan in that slinky black dress and sitting in one of the finest restaurants in Houston, he'd decided that she outshone every other woman by far.

She was bright, funny and personable. Even out of her element, she maintained a down-home quality to her. But she was versatile enough to fit in with a swankier crowd.

Unlike most of the others, she hadn't placed any demands on the waiter. She'd also tried to make Peyton feel better about Henri referring to him as Mr. Jenkins—another close call, although he was just about to tell her himself. And she'd even shown kindness and respect to a homeless man on the street.

As they passed through the revolving glass doors and into the lobby of the boutique hotel Zoe had booked for them, he tightened his grip on her waist.

He usually stayed in a corporate apartment when he was in Houston, but he hadn't wanted to take her there. He'd wanted to stay somewhere more impressive, someplace where he'd have room service and a full staff at his beck and call.

When they entered the mirrored elevator, he realized how easy it would be to take her in his arms and kiss her with all the longing he'd stored up this past week. But Megan wasn't just any woman he'd wined and dined in the past. She was special.

She wasn't someone to take to bed, then have Zoe send flowers to the next day as a parting gift while he flew out of town on his new Gulfstream.

And right now, as she gazed at him with those pretty caramel-colored eyes, he wasn't sure how or when or even *if* he'd handle their parting. All he knew was that he was flirting with a passion he could hardly contain.

When the elevator door opened, they headed down the hall to their adjoining rooms. He'd never been faced with a situation like this before. In the past, he'd always known how his other nights would end up as he made his way down a hotel corridor with a dinner date.

But now? He had no idea. He could tell her the truth about himself now, and once she got over her initial shock or anger at him for not coming clean sooner, she'd soften up. She'd see him as a kindhearted, generous man who cared deeply about her. A man who was falling in love with her, if he hadn't done so already.

She'd also realize that he was as rich as they came, and that he could buy her whatever her heart desired, take her to any exotic location she might want to travel to. He could invite her to come to his room for a nightcap, to share his bed tonight. But would she come because of what he could offer her?

Or because of who he really was—and how she felt about that man?

There was only one way to find out. And that was to hold onto his secret until after she'd let him know how she felt about Peyton—or at least, how she felt about getting romantically involved with him.

So the ball, or rather, the rest of the night, was in her court.

When they stopped in front of the door to her room, she turned to face him. "Thank you."

"For what?" He wanted to kick himself for responding with such a stupid question, but it was the only response he could come up with. Clearly she meant their date and all he'd done to impress her.

"For dinner and an amazing evening, of course. But also for helping us in the shop and for being so understanding with Tyler. And, well, thank you for…everything." She glanced at both doors, then back at him.

She seemed to be weighing a decision, and he truly

wanted it to be hers alone. But he couldn't help edging her toward the more advantageous choice.

"And for this?" He leaned down and placed his lips gently against hers.

Apparently, that was all the convincing she needed, because she slanted her mouth over his and slipped her arms around his neck. He pulled her close, and within moments they were making out in the hallway like a couple of teenagers with no place to go.

He used his tongue to explore her mouth, as his hands sought out every inch of her waist, back and hips.

Somehow they ended up leaning against the wall. He ran his fingers through that luscious head of red curls that had been the source of many fantasies for him over the past few weeks.

As the elevator doors opened and another hotel guest entered the hall, they both pulled back, eyes wide, lips parted, breaths coming out in raspy pants.

They averted their gazes until the man passed them and let himself into his own room.

Then Clay pulled his key card out of his pocket. "Should we…?"

"Yes. But do you have any…um…?" She glanced down before looking back at him with pink cheeks.

He assumed she was asking about protection. Fortunately, he'd picked up a box of condoms in the little newsstand shop off the lobby while he'd waited for her to come downstairs and meet him for dinner. He didn't want her to think he'd been too presumptuous, so he just nodded in response.

She nodded back, and the decision was made.

He opened the door to the room, led her inside, then pulled her into his arms. As she slipped into his embrace, she drew his lips to hers, and their bodies took up right where they'd left off, stroking, caressing, exploring.

The kiss in the hallway had fueled their passion, and now that they were alone and behind closed doors, the intensity of their desire built until they were both on fire.

Clay took her by the hand and led her to the bed, where he kissed her again. As if eager to feel her bare skin against his, she reached for the zipper on her dress, tugging and struggling just a bit.

He helped her finish the chore, sliding the garment over her shoulders as she shimmied out of it. When it dropped to the floor, she kicked it to the side.

As she stood before him in a black lacy bra and matching panties, a sexy ensemble he never would have guessed she'd worn under that classy dress, his heart soared, and his blood raced. Her body, petite yet lithe, was everything he'd imagined it to be and more. And tonight she was his.

Following her lead, he removed his clothes and eased toward her. She skimmed her nails across his chest, sending a shiver through his veins and a rush of heat through his blood. Then she unsnapped her bra and freed her breasts, full and round, the dusky pink tips peaked and begging to be touched..

He took a nipple in his mouth, lavishing first one and then the other until she swayed and clutched his shoulder to stay balanced.

But why remain standing? He lifted her on to the bed. As all that gorgeous red hair he'd mussed with his fingers now splayed out over the pillow, he took a moment to drink in the luscious sight.

"You're more beautiful than I'd ever imagined, Megan."

A slow smile stretched across her lips. "So are you."

She found the man inside of him attractive. Not his name or his money or his holdings. Determined to ensure that she'd feel the same way when he revealed the truth, he joined her on the bed.

After using the condom to protect them, he entered her. And as her body responded to his, arching and meeting his thrusts, taking and giving, nothing mattered but the two of them. When they both reached a peak, she cried out. He shuddered, releasing with her in an amazing sexual explosion. Talk about fireworks....

Making love with Megan had been all that he'd hoped for and more. And as he held her close, riding the ebb and flow, he wondered when to tell her that she'd just knocked it out of the park with Clay Jenkins, a man who could not only take her to the moon but buy it for her.

Should he tell her now? Or wait until breakfast?

As she snuggled in his arms, as they basked in what could be described only as a perfect afterglow, she whispered, "Oh, Peyton..."

And breakfast won out.

The clock on the nightstand read 7:25 a.m. While Peyton showered, Megan stretched out in the luxurious hotel bed, savoring the greatest night of lovemaking she'd ever had and running her foot along an expanse of sheets with what had to be the highest thread count she'd ever slept in. The sheer decadence made her want to call Peyton out from the steamy bathroom to partake in the silky smoothness with her.

They'd made love with urgency last night, then with

slow excitement and awareness this morning. Peyton was an incredible lover, and she could get used to waking up in his arms.

She could also be tempted to call Caroline and tell her something had come up and she wouldn't be able to get the kids until midday. After all, checkout wasn't until eleven. But they had a long drive back to Brighton Valley, and Peyton had to open the shop. She also needed to get her jams and preserves ready for her booth at the farmers' market tomorrow.

For that reason, Peyton had asked her to order them both something for breakfast before he'd kissed her and hopped into the shower. So she studied the room service menu and placed the call, hoping she hadn't chosen too much. But he'd said he was hungry, and so was she.

When he came out of the bathroom, they changed places. And by the time she'd showered and walked out in one of the fluffy hotel robes, a waiter was wheeling in their breakfast on a white linen-covered table.

Peyton tipped the man. Then, when they were alone, he pulled out a chair for her.

"I've never had room service before." Had she just admitted that? Great, now she sounded like the inexperienced country hick she'd feared he'd see her as.

"You should have someone cook for you and serve you—and often." He winked, and her heart did a flip-flop.

Was he implying there would be more dates like this one?

"I hope I didn't order too much food. I knew you liked bacon and eggs, as well as biscuits with gravy. But you also have a weakness for pastries."

He reached over and squeezed her knee, which had

slipped out of the robe, then gave it a sensuous caress. "That's something that amazes me about you. You have a knack for knowing exactly what I want and when I want it. It's like an instinct."

"Ha." Todd had told her that she never understood a man's needs. "My ex-husband would disagree with you."

Oops, she hadn't meant to bring him up. That was certainly a buzzkill.

"I'm sure there are probably a lot of things your ex and I wouldn't agree on."

She smiled, but an awkward silence had already filled the room.

"Was it always bad between the two of you?" Peyton asked.

Megan wondered if he was comparing himself to her ex-husband, and while she didn't want to talk about it, she didn't want Peyton to think that she was lacking as a wife or to think that a relationship with her would end with the same result.

"Things were exciting at first, but we were so young and had no idea what the real world was like. I was mortified when I got pregnant while we were in high school, but I convinced myself that if I tried hard enough, then we'd be okay. But college was a difficult transition for him and married life was even tougher. He was used to being the big fish in a small pond. And when he only made second string, it really got to him. And his ego took a beating."

Megan stole a glance at Peyton, and his expression urged her to go on.

"After a while, it seemed that he spent more time with his teammates and at the gym—or so he said. It didn't take a bloodhound to smell the alcohol on his breath. But I adored Tyler and was determined to make our family work. After graduation his football career was already in the tank, so he took a job in Houston, and we moved to the suburbs. Lisa was born a year later."

"I take it things didn't get better away from the university."

"No, it only got worse. He once told me that I poured all of my heart into the home and the children and that I was no fun anymore, that I didn't care about him. It seemed that the harder I tried, the more distant he became. Before long he came home so late at night that I didn't even bother to keep his dinner warm anymore. It was getting more apparent that divorce was in our future, but I wasn't raised that way and didn't want to think I'd failed at having a family."

"How could you ever think you were the one who'd failed?"

"Looking back, I can see that it was his problems, his insecurities and issues that led to our divorce. I was just coming to that conclusion when I received a phone call from a woman claiming to be his lover. Even though I knew the marriage was beyond salvaging, that revelation merely set off a series of events that let me know our whole marriage had been racked with lies."

"I don't understand."

"Finding out about his wealthy girlfriend or a whole laundry list of other mistresses wasn't the hardest part of our divorce."

Peyton's arched brow questioned her last comment.

"You see, his irresponsible lifestyle and spending habits had done a real number on our finances. I'd been so caught up with caring for the house and the children that I let him handle the checkbook—actually, he insisted, and I didn't argue. But that proved to be a big mistake. I had no idea how far in debt he'd gotten us. In the end, I had no choice but to file for bankruptcy, which left me in a real bind, and he's seen no reason to help me financially."

"Where is he now? Why isn't he sending you any money for the kids?"

"The court ordered him to pay child support, but before he'd written three checks, he left the state with that other woman and hasn't been heard from since. I guess with a rich lover to fund his spending habits, he no longer needed his grandfather—a man who'd doled out more cash to his family than hugs."

"I can't believe he wouldn't want to support his kids."

"He figured I'd go to his family and ask for help, knowing his grandpa would contribute what he should be paying himself, but I refused to do it. I decided that, by letting his arrears mount up in court, eventually he'll have to be held accountable to someone."

"In the meantime, you suffer financially."

"It's not so bad. I'm getting by okay."

Peyton clucked his tongue. "What an ass. Stepping out on you like that."

"You know, by the time I found out about the other woman, I wasn't even really that upset. I'd fallen out of love with him by then, so I was never really jealous. It was the lying and sneaking that broke my heart. I've always hated liars. They're the most despicable and cowardly people. Why couldn't he have just come to me and told me that he stopped loving me, that the marriage wasn't working for him? I could have handled the truth. What I couldn't stomach was the lies and the deceit."

Peyton grew silent—stone-cold quiet.

Apparently he didn't have an answer for that. Or more likely, he was uncomfortable with the direction the conversation had taken.

Megan kicked herself again for bringing it up, especially now. But heck, he'd asked the questions. And he'd appeared to be interested.

But maybe it was too much information too soon.

Somehow she needed to lighten things up. "Anyway, I got some job training after I moved back to Brighton Valley. And thanks to my jams and muffins, plus the extra income and the health insurance I receive from Zorba's, I'm finally starting to see some light at the end of the financial tunnel." And in case he thought she'd gotten too attached to him, she added, "The kids and I are doing just fine on our own."

She dug into her scrambled eggs. As they ate, he remained quiet. She chalked it up to his focus on the delicious spread before them, but after a few minutes, she asked, "Is something wrong?"

Wrong? Hell, yes. But Clay couldn't admit that. So he said, "No, not at all."

He'd meant to confess his identity this morning, before taking her back to Brighton Valley. He'd planned to spring the news as a surprise. He'd thought that after a fine dinner and an amazing night of lovemaking, he would swoop in like Prince Charming and give her all the things she'd ever wanted.

He'd thought that she'd be pleased to know that all her financial worries were over.

But if all she'd ever wanted was a guy who was hon-

est and up front, especially about who he really was...
then maybe now wasn't the time to tell her.

"These pastries are good," he said, "but not as good
as yours."

She smiled. "Thanks."

Hopefully she hadn't picked up on his guilt or his
reason for feeling that way. He'd tell her, of course, and
rid himself of that dark cloud that now hovered over
him—over them.

But he couldn't very well make his confession on the
tail end of a revelation like that, especially when she'd
professed how much she hated liars.

Still, he had to do it soon—before he tripped up or
she found out before he had a chance to tell her himself.

Chapter Eleven

Clay hadn't seen much of Megan after their night in Houston. The excuse he gave her, as well as himself, was that she needed to get ready for the farmers' market. But that was a load of bull, and as Saturday afternoon wore on, he began to feel like a real jerk.

By Sunday the guilt had really kicked in, and he couldn't help thinking that he deserved whatever happened once he told her the truth. Finally, when he couldn't stand it any longer, he took a shower, got dressed and fixed a light breakfast. Then he walked to the town square in search of the booth where she'd set up her jams and preserves.

He'd offered to drive over to her place and help her load her stepdad's truck with her wares, but she'd said that she had it covered and that he didn't need to bother. He'd agreed to let her and Tyler handle it on their own, but now he wished he had insisted.

At a quarter to nine, Clay found her booth, which she'd decorated with a red-checkered tablecloth, wooden crates and baskets of homemade muffins.

She looked adorable in denim jeans and a fitted white blouse, with her hair pulled back in a ponytail. But she was busy talking to a woman and her daughter about one of her preserves when he walked up, so he didn't greet her with a hug or a kiss.

And that merely made him feel even more awkward than he already did.

Damn, if he had a tail, it would've been tucked between his legs. He'd waited long enough to tell her who he was. Dragging his feet wasn't helping, and the sooner he got it over with, the better he'd feel, even if it angered her. After all, Peyton might have wooed her, but Clay had a way of keeping women around. Surely she'd get over it once she realized who he was and what he could give her.

After the woman made a purchase and walked off with her daughter, Megan spotted him, and their gazes met. Her smile nearly did him in—in part because he hoped she'd still look at him that way after he told her he'd been stringing her along for weeks even though he hadn't needed to.

"How's it going?" he asked.

"It was a little slow at first, but things have really picked up." She reached under the table and pulled out a foil-covered package. "I made you a breakfast burrito. I thought you might not take the time to eat."

She was always thinking about him. "Thanks. As a matter of fact, I'm starving. But listen, I really need to talk to you. Can you take a break?"

Megan gave him a little shrug and smiled. "I usually sell out by noon. Is that soon enough?"

He supposed it would have to be. "Sure."

Before she could respond, a middle-aged man wearing a pair of khaki slacks, a blue button-down shirt and a navy blue sports jacket stopped by the booth.

"Are you Megan Adams?" he asked.

"Yes, I am."

He reached into his lapel and pulled out a business card. "I'm Harvey Swenson with Fowler Markets, a retail chain out of Dallas. While passing through town a couple of weeks ago, I stopped at Caroline's Diner and had the pleasure of tasting your spicy peach preserve, the one you make with jalapeño chilies. It was so delicious I wanted to take a jar home with me, but the waitress told me they didn't have any left. In fact, they always sell out of it early."

"I'm glad you enjoyed it, Mr. Swenson. If you'd like to take some with you today, I have a couple of jars left. I'm afraid it's the first thing I run out of at the farmers' market, too. I can't seem to keep it in stock."

"That doesn't surprise me. Anyway, I was wondering if you'd be interested in selling your recipe."

"I'm sorry," she said. "It's been in the family for years, so it's not for sale."

"I figured you'd say that." The man grinned. "But I'll take all you have left, as well as several jars of each of your other jams and jellies."

While Megan proceeded to bag the man's order and total up the sale, Clay scanned the crowd of locals who'd gathered on a Sunday morning to roam the booths, looking at homemade quilts, produce, artwork and all the other things people had either made or brought to sell.

He suspected the town square would really get hopping once the community church let out.

As Mr. Swenson walked off, another man approached. This one Clay recognized. It was Travis Bellingham, a guy he'd gone to school with at Washington High.

Travis had been one of Todd Redding's friends, one of the jocks who'd harassed him when he'd been a freshman. He stiffened, wondering if Travis would recognize him, even though he doubted that he would.

"Hey," Travis said to Megan. "How's it going?"

"Not bad." She straightened and placed her hands on her hips. "And you?"

"I'm all right. My dad took sick, so I had to come home and help out my mom on the ranch."

"I'm sorry to hear that." Megan reached for a jar of plum jelly. "Give this to your dad. He used to stop by the booth regularly. I wondered why I hadn't seen him lately."

"Thanks. I'm sure he'll appreciate it."

Megan turned to Clay. "Travis, this is Peyton Johnson. He and I've been working together at Zorba the Geek's."

As the men shook hands, Megan added, "Travis and my ex-husband were good friends. They played football together in high school."

"Yeah," Travis said. "But I never was good enough to get a college scholarship like Todd did."

Todd?

Clay's gut tightened. No, it couldn't be. Megan had dated a football player—and a quarterback. But she'd gone to Brighton Valley, not Washington High. And Clay had just assumed that the guy…

Hell, her last name was Adams. Maybe the only co-incidence was that she'd dated and married a football player at BVHS whose first name was Todd.

When Travis had taken the gift jar of jelly and left, Clay asked, "So that was your ex-husband's friend?"

"Yes."

The knot in his gut twisted. "And you went to school with both of them . . . .?"

"No, Todd attended Washington High. What I didn't realize then but found out later was that he'd conquered most of the girls at his school. So he decided to move on to newer pickings in Brighton Valley, where no one knew of his reputation as a love-'em-and-leave-'em type. Since I'd been busy helping my mom with the orchard and with chores at home, I hadn't dated much. What can I say? He was a charmer, and by the time graduation rolled around, I was pregnant."

So Megan was the girl Todd Redding had gotten pregnant and married?

"He must have loved you," Clay said.

"He said he did, but he'd been offered a partial athletic scholarship at a college in Houston, and he was pretty upset about the pregnancy. He didn't want me to have the baby, but I couldn't do that."

"So he married you," Clay said.

"Not without a lot of pressure from his family, especially his grandfather, who insisted that he 'do the right thing.' And being young and naive, I believed love would solve a slew of problems. So I agreed." She scanned the crowd, probably looking for eavesdroppers—or, more likely, the kids—then continued. "We got married at the end of June and stayed with his parents until it was time to move to Houston. Thankfully,

Todd's grandfather was able to supplement the scholarship so we could afford to live on campus in married housing. I'd never been one of the studious kids, so I was uncomfortable living in a college setting, but I made the best of it."

Clay probably ought to say something, but he had no idea what. And even if he did, his gut was twisting something awful. He'd known her ex was a football player, that he'd been a jerk....

She looked at him, a shadow dimming the light that had once brightened her eyes. "You pretty much know the rest."

Yes, he did. But he hadn't realized that her ex-husband had been Todd Redding, his high school nemesis. "Listen, if you don't mind, I'm going to look around and check out the rest of the market."

"Okay. I'm not going anywhere."

He tossed her a smile, then took off, eager to put some distance between them. He just needed time to reassess what it all meant to him.

Sure, he cared about Megan. He might even love her. But did he really want to get involved with Todd Redding's family? He hated Todd, and the last thing he wanted was to associate Megan with the guy who had made his teen years a living hell.

Did he really want what Todd had left behind? What if Todd came back someday and wanted them back? Where would that leave Clay?

Did he want to come clean at all? If he made his excuses and left Brighton Valley now, hiding behind the geeky kid who still lurked inside him, he could keep his secret and his dignity.

Besides, in his experience, the girls who'd gone for Todd never would have settled for someone like Clay.

Megan sold out of her jams and jellies right after lunch, so there wasn't any reason to hang out in town square much longer. The chamber of commerce, who'd set up the event, had asked the venders not to tear down the booths until after two, but she could certainly put a sign out for customers and then slip off to find the kids and Peyton.

The only problem was, the kids had been checking in with her off and on, but Peyton had been pretty scarce.

Why was that?

There could be only one reason. He regretted their lovemaking.

Disappointment poured over her, making it difficult to hold her chin up and keep a smile on her face. But she tried to shake it off. After all, she'd known nothing would come of a relationship with Peyton. He'd be leaving town soon. In fact, he might even be packing now. Was that where he'd gone?

Just as she'd regretted getting intimate with Todd back when they'd been in high school, she was feeling that same way about Peyton now. Making love with him, as wonderful as it had been—was a mistake. He'd pulled back—no matter how kind he might have been, how different from Todd he might be—and her only defense at this point was to withdraw, too. And to pretend as though nothing was wrong.

So she gathered up the kids and told them they were going home. There she would lick her wounds. All the while, she would try to put on a happy face so that Lisa and Tyler wouldn't know how badly she hurt.

Apparently, the ploy worked because they jabbered between the two of them all the way home, which she really didn't mind. The buzz of the sibling banter allowed her to keep her melancholy mood to herself.

Once back at the farm, she told the children that she'd unload the truck herself.

"Cool," Tyler said. "I'm going to work on my report."

As the kids scampered off, leaving her to mull over the bittersweet memory of the one amazing night she'd spent with Peyton, she placed the broken-down parts to her booth into the shed in back of the house.

She assumed the relationship was over. She'd probably dashed it all by talking too much about Todd the morning after. But maybe that was for the best. What would have become of her and Peyton anyway?

Still, a small part of her would grieve for what could have been because, like it or not, she'd come to care for Peyton.

Care for him? She may have even come to love him.

Once the truck was unloaded and parked back by the barn, she entered the kitchen, washed her hands and prepared to fix dinner. She decided on meat loaf, mashed potatoes and green beans.

She'd no more than pulled the ground beef from the refrigerator when Tyler called out, "Mom, come here!"

"I'm busy," she hollered back. "You'll need to come into the kitchen if you want to talk to me."

"But you gotta see this. And it's on the computer screen. I can't bring it to you."

"What is it?" she asked, not the least bit interested in looking at whatever he felt compelled to show her.

"It's a picture of Clay Jenkins, the head of Geekon Enterprises. And he looks a whole lot like Peyton. If you take off his glasses and shave his beard, the two of them could be brothers. Or maybe even *twins*."

The CEO of Geekon Enterprises? No, it couldn't be. But her interest was definitely piqued, and she left the package of meat, the carton of eggs and the mixing bowl on the kitchen counter.

As she started toward the den, Tyler called out, "OMG. It really *is* him. And I can prove it."

Megan's senses reeled, and she wasn't sure what moved faster, her feet or her mind, as she hurried to see what Tyler had uncovered.

"What did you find?" she asked her son as she stepped in front of the computer screen.

"I was doing my report on Bill Gates but decided to do some research on Clay Jenkins just because I was curious about him. And I was looking at photos of him. I thought he looked a lot like Peyton. And then I found this."

It was a series of photos taken of Clayton Jenkins over the years, showing the metamorphosis of the geeky teenager to the stylish, mega-rich software mogul.

Her heart stood still, then dropped into the pit of her stomach, setting off an emotional metamorphosis of its own—from shock to disbelief to flat-out anger.

It hadn't been her talking about Todd that had silenced him yesterday. It had been her pointing out her disgust of liars and men she couldn't trust.

The jerk had felt guilty. And he darn well should have.

Even when she'd poured out her own heart and soul to him, he still hadn't had the decency to tell her the truth.

And just like Todd, he'd taken her to bed, sharing

the most intimate act between a man and a woman, but all the while she'd given herself freely to him, he'd held something back from her.

He'd hidden the man he really was.

When Clay saw that Megan had left town square early yesterday, he figured she'd sold out and had driven back to the farm. He'd used the time away from her to think about things, but he hadn't come to any conclusions. He'd expected to hear from her eventually, since women tended to chase after him and he'd never had to pursue them.

But by evening he hadn't heard from her, so he figured he'd better call. But he still wasn't sure what to say. He continued to struggle with the dilemma until the hours before dawn.

Finally, as he woke up alone in the small, empty apartment and headed downstairs to the shop, which they'd cleaned and organized together, his thoughts came together.

In spite of the fame and fortune, his life was small and empty. He'd been missing something all along— something that he'd found in Megan.

He'd never felt so warm, so loved, so complete until he'd returned to Brighton Valley, stripped off the Clay Jenkins persona and let Peyton Johnson take the helm.

In a way, Peyton was the real him—not the geeky kid who'd struggled to be loved and accepted or the CEO who could buy himself fame and a place in the world.

And Clay had to show Megan that he was all three people—the kid, the man and the CEO—all wrapped up into one messed-up package who loved her more than he knew how to admit.

Yep, that was what he'd do. Then he'd ask her to marry him and move to Silicon Valley. And if she'd rather live elsewhere, that was fine with him. It was her choice. He would make it happen for her.

He was just about to place a long-overdue phone call when he heard a key turn in the lock on the front door of the shop. He assumed it was her arriving at work early, which was good. His confession would take some time, and he'd like to keep that closed sign up for as long as it took.

But when Megan stepped through the door, she wasn't wearing a smile or carrying a foil-wrapped breakfast treat.

"You lied to me," she said. The fire that lit her eyes damn near nailed him to the wall, and he knew that she'd learned the truth on her own.

"I can explain."

"Don't bother, *Mr. Jenkins*. I don't want to hear anything you have to say."

Then, before he could try and say anything else to smooth things over, like beg her to listen to his reason for maintaining a secret identity, which no longer seemed to hold an ounce of water, she turned on her heel, walked out of the shop and slammed the door so hard the bell clanged to the floor and rolled to his feet.

Clay stood there for the longest time, trying to make sense of it all. Her anger he could understand. But his pain and the crushing disappointment had sideswiped him, and he wasn't sure what to do about it.

In the past, he could pick up a phone and call Zoe. With all the money at his disposal, his creative executive assistant was able to make any number of things happen for him.

But something told him he'd just lost the one thing he wanted and needed more than anything else in the world. And there wasn't any way he was going to be able to buy her or coax her back.

Megan cried all the way back to the farm. When the kids had asked why they weren't going to their summer programs today, she'd given them the reason she'd always hated to hear as a child: "Just because."

But she couldn't very well tell them that she had to drive into town earlier than the program started and that she wanted to be alone when she did it. Nor did she want to explain why she wasn't going into work today—or ever again.

Tyler, of course, had figured it out.

"Are you mad at Mr. Johnson—I mean, Mr. Jenkins?" he asked.

"He lied to us. And there was no reason for it."

The boy merely dropped his head.

They sat on the living room sofa for nearly thirty minutes, lost in their thoughts, their disappointment, their sadness. The ringing of the telephone finally drew Megan from hers.

She reached for the receiver, snatched it from the cradle and answered. "Hello?"

"Ms. Adams?"

"Yes."

"This is Harvey Swenson with Fowler Markets, the retail chain out of Dallas. We talked at the farmers' market yesterday."

"Yes, Mr. Swenson. What can I do for you?"

"Well, Ms. Adams, it's what I'd like to do for you. I told our CEO, George Fowler, about your products after I'd tasted them at Caroline's Diner a while back. And then I presented them to him early this morning, after buying them yesterday. And he'd like to sell them in our stores. So we're prepared to make you an offer."

"Like I said before, I'm not willing to sell the recipe."

"No, we understand that. We'd like to purchase the product. You'd hold all rights. You'd be in business for yourself—we'd just like an exclusive right to sell your jams, jellies and preserves through our stores. So what do you say?"

This was the break she needed. Her financial troubles were going to be a thing of the past.

"I'm definitely interested, Mr. Swenson."

"Good. We'd like to talk more with you in Dallas on Monday, the seventh of July. Are you available?"

"Yes, I can be."

"Good. I'll set up the meeting with our board of directors and then give you the details later. Welcome to the Fowler family, Ms. Adams. I think this is going to be a very lucrative venture for you."

She certainly hoped so. It was time for her luck to turn. And maybe it would help her heart to heal, too. She hadn't needed Todd Redding or his family money.

And she didn't need Clay Jenkins, either.

Chapter Twelve

Clay hadn't realized how much he would miss having Megan—or her homey touches—in the shop until he'd had to spend ten days without her. But he was running things at Zorba's until Don came back from vacation.

The doctor had released the man to return to work, but Clay had figured an all-expenses-paid trip to San Antonio to visit family would be a nice break for the couple, especially since Cindy had finally finished her last round of chemo.

With one phone call to Zoe, he could have had corporate send a temporary replacement manager here in less than a day, but abandoning the shop now would be akin to giving up, and he wasn't a quitter.

Besides, he had something to prove—not just to Megan, who might never forgive him, but to himself.

Funny thing, though. Everyone in Brighton Valley

now knew who he was, thanks to the confession he'd made to the Carpenters and later to Sally at the diner. Yet they weren't treating him too much differently than they had when they'd known him as Peyton Johnson. In fact, because he was once one of them before he'd made it big—or so they'd figured—they seemed to have embraced him.

He supposed that he owed a lot of that to Megan, who hadn't gone around telling everyone that he was a lying jerk. She'd kept her anger and her assessment to herself. And that made him love and respect her even more. It also made him feel even worse about deceiving her and more determined to prove that she could put her trust in him again someday.

As he sat behind one of the last computers left to repair, putting the panel back onto the hard drive he'd just rewired, the reattached bell on the front door jangled.

"Be right with you," he called out.

He wiped his hands on his jeans, which he'd started wearing when he realized he no longer had to hide his identity in town or impress anyone by looking like a corporate bigwig.

When he made his way to the front of the store, he spotted the Franco sisters at the counter, the two elderly women who'd been eating at Caroline's Diner the first day he'd arrived in town.

"Morning, Clay," said the one wearing a light pink blouse.

"Hello, ladies. What brings you into Zorba's today?"

"Sister and I were in the grocery last week," the one in blue said, "and we heard y'all have them laptop computer gizmos for sale down here for one hundred dollars."

Sister, the one in pink, nodded to confirm this.

Clay wanted to kick himself for ever making that crazy deal with Riley. At this point, nearly every citizen in Brighton Valley had picked up a thousand-dollar laptop for a tenth of the price. But there was no way he'd refuse the Franco sisters the same deal, especially when he knew they were on such a limited income.

"Unfortunately, that special ended. But just between the three of us, I happen to have one of those special-deal computers set aside for a fellow who never came to pick it up. So I can let you have it at the same price."

"See?" the one in pink said. "I told you he was a good man, sister. He didn't have to offer us that deal. He could have put that machine right back on the shelf and sold it to someone else at full price. But no, he didn't. He let you and me have it."

"You did at that. 'Course, I was the one who recognized him from that old magazine I saw down at the Laundromat. And I told you he was rich as old fury. Didn't I, sister?"

"Yes, you did. You also said he looked a lot like that boy who worked here with Ralph several years ago, but I thought you were going daffy on me, just like poor Aunt Thelma."

Clay cleared his throat. "So do each of you need a laptop?"

"Oh, no, dear," the pink sister said. "Just one will do." She placed a liver-spotted hand on the other woman's shoulder. "We share everything."

"All right. That's good." Clay couldn't imagine the Franco sisters needing all the bells and whistles or the ultra-storage capacity of the Geekon Blast. "Now, in order to get you the best machine, what exactly are you looking to do on your laptop?"

"We mostly want it for getting emails and pictures and whatnot from our nephew out in Washington and our cousin in Des Moines. And then sister likes to tinker in the garden."

The blue sister, he realized, would be the gardener.

"Mrs. Fosley down at the library said she can get lots of good gardening articles off of that internet place. I like to get my papers every week, but our house is so small I feel like I'm running out of room with the way they can all stack up like they do. Someone said we can get them on a reader-e. So we'd need a reader-e feature."

"You mean an e-reader?" He tried not to chuckle.

"Is that the same thing we can get our books on?" the pink sister asked. "After Glenda's bookstore closed, we haven't been able to find our favorite romance novels. And the library doesn't stock enough."

"The library doesn't have enough books?" he asked.

"Not romance. And that's what we love to read. Don't you favor a good romance?"

He certainly would, but he'd pretty much crashed and burned in the only one that had meant anything to him, although he was doing his best to get back in Megan's good graces, even if he was starting at the bottom and working his way up. "I guess I'd better read more books."

"It would certainly help, although you're a nice looking fellow with lots of money. I'd think the gals would be fighting to have a chance to date you."

Not the one he really wanted.

"What's wrong with Megan?" the Franco sister wearing blue asked. "She's the little redhead who works here. She'd be a fine match for any man. She's pretty and a good cook."

Her sister gave her a nudge with her elbow. "She's got children, and a lot of bachelors aren't interested in dating women with children, even if they would make a fine wife."

"Just for the record," Clay said, "I am interested in Megan. And there's not a thing wrong with her. She's perfect. And she'd make a fine wife. She's also a wonderful mother, and that makes her even more appealing—strange as that might sound to you or to other bachelors. And it wouldn't bother me a bit if you spread that piece of news around town."

At that, the sisters giggled.

"As for the e-reader," Clay said, "you can also get your books on them."

"That's what we hear," the pink sister said. "But we don't know the first thing about 'em."

As he went over technology basics with the Franco sisters, he realized there was a market not only for computer classes but also for affordable and simple user-friendly e-readers for folks who wanted to download books by their favorite authors, dabble in emails and search the internet but weren't fully committed to diving into the digital age.

When the ladies pulled out their coin purses to start counting out their quarters and carefully folded one-dollar bills, Clay didn't wait for them to get to fifty.

He told himself it was a businessman's impatience and not his generosity that made him refuse their money. But he was embracing the new Brighton Valley version of Clay Jenkins, who was now wearing jeans and giving away laptops to dear old ladies for almost nothing.

The sister in pink nudged the one in blue. "I told you he was a good man."

"You sure did. And now, with the money we saved, we can donate to the Brighton Valley town council so those scrooges will reinstate the fireworks."

Clay had forgotten that the big Fourth of July festivities would take place on Friday. The parade and festival would be followed by a fireworks show, which had always been one of his favorite summer memories when he'd worked here.

He'd enjoyed getting lost in the crowd and blending in with the locals. Plus, he'd always been a sucker for pyrotechnic displays and booming colors in the night sky. But what had the sister in blue said about the town council not providing fireworks this year?

"We've lived here all our lives and this will be the first time in more than eighty years that they haven't had the money set aside to pay for the fireworks. It's a shame."

"A real shame, sister. But maybe if enough of us donate, the town can afford a few rockets and airbombs and bangers. If not, we can have Mr. Perkins drive us over to the next county to see if we can find that firecracker stand outside of town so we can set a few off ourselves."

Clay had no idea how the two elderly sisters knew the terminology, but it was a little unsettling to think of them trying to set off their own illegal display.

He bit his tongue until the ladies shuffled out of the store. Then he looked up the number for city hall and placed a call. When he told the receptionist his name, it took her only a minute to connect him to the mayor's cell phone.

He was finally fitting in around town and didn't like drawing attention to himself, but he wasn't afraid to use his status when he wanted to get something done.

"What can I do for you Mr. Johnson...I mean Jenkins?"

Boy, it would take some time to live that down.

"Please, call me Clay." Without waiting for the mayor to call him anything, he cut to the chase. "Listen, I heard there was a funding issue with the fireworks show."

"Well, to be honest, the town council has a tight budget this year with the way the economy is and all. They put in that new lighting at the Little League field. And they had to vote on whether to pay for new computers for the elementary computer lab or to use the money for the fireworks display. Needless to say, the students come first. I know it's a big letdown for the townspeople, but we're still having the summer festival and the parade. And there will be buses to take people over to Wexler to see their fireworks show."

Clay thought about the town of Wexler and how it had never felt like home. He didn't like to think of them one-upping Brighton Valley with their Fourth of July festivities.

"How much does it cost to put on a good fireworks show?"

"Normally, the council spends about twenty thousand."

"Suppose an anonymous donor was willing to be a sponsor for the event? Is it too late to put the show together before this weekend?"

"I suppose if this anonymous donor also happened to be one of the most famous anonymous computer entrepreneurs of our time and had enough anonymous connections, we could get the anonymous ball rolling anytime you say so."

Clay could almost see the man grinning through the phone, teasing with him as if he were a regular Brighton Valley resident and not some mega-millionaire who could buy and sell this town ten times over.

"I'll tell you what. Geekon will contribute fifteen thousand dollars toward the fireworks. And we'll also donate the computers to the school."

"That's very generous, Clay."

"I'm glad to help. Besides, I messed up with Megan Adams and I know there's not a lot of hope for me with her. But I wouldn't mind having her think that I do have *some* redeeming qualities. So if you can spread the word around town that I'm an upright guy and well-intentioned, Geekon will also throw in some tablets and printers for the school while we're at it."

"I think most of the town already knows that about you, Clay. And although I'm happily married, I still won't pretend to understand how my wife's mind works. But I can tell you this. Women have their pride, and actions speak louder than words. So I'll put in a good word for you, but you're going to need to stick around and convince Megan yourself. I can tell you that my own proposal came after a bit of heartfelt groveling."

When the call had ended, Clay emailed Zoe to give her a heads-up on what he'd promised so she could start the ball rolling and call the mayor to find out where to send the check.

Clay and Zoe had kept in touch daily over the past few weeks, and he'd been amazed at how well Geekon Enterprises had been running in his absence.

He'd chosen a good team, and it was good to know

that he could run the corporation from wherever he decided to put down roots.

As he looked out over Main Street, he felt those roots taking a firmer hold. He was really beginning to like this town, as well as the people in it—everyone from the Franco sisters to Sally at the diner to Mayor Mendez.

Plus, now that he'd reconnected with Rick, it was nice to have a sense of belonging, maybe for the first time. And to feel as though he'd finally come home, even if it was just an apartment over the shop.

If only he could reconcile with Megan, she and the kids would be the icing on the cake, the family he'd always longed to have.

A familiar face passed by the glass window, and before Clay could run out onto the street, Tyler opened the door and made his way inside.

"It's good to see you," Clay said.

Tyler gave him a nod. "Hey."

The boy appeared a little nervous, as though he might want to tear into Clay for lying, too. And if he needed to get it off his chest, then so be it. Clay figured he owed him that much, and that he might as well make it easy on him.

"What are you up to?" he asked.

"Lisa has another game at the park. I just kinda missed the shop and wanted to stop by and see the computers and stuff."

Clay could certainly understand that. He wondered if Megan would be okay with her son talking to the last man she probably ever wanted to see again. "Does your mom know you're here?"

"I told her I was going for a walk. She knows I hate

going to those boring sports games. So what's up? You got any new computers in?"

"No, not yet. But Geekon is going to donate some new ones to the computer lab at the school. And some tablets and printers, too." Clay knew he sounded pathetic and that the boy had to know he was trying to buy himself back into his good graces.

Tyler simply scuffed the toe of his sneaker along the worn carpet.

Clay tried a different approach. "You know, Tyler, I'm really sorry about everything that went down between me and your mom. A lot of it is grown-up stuff, and I can't expect you to understand. But I never meant to lie to her or to any of you about who I was."

"So then why did you? I would have liked you just fine if you would have told us that you were *the* Clay Jenkins."

"See, that's thing. I didn't want people liking me just because I was Clay Jenkins."

"Why?"

"Because when you have a lot of money or a lot of power, sometimes people treat you differently and don't always act like themselves. I just wanted people to think I was normal."

"I guess that makes sense. Sometimes I wish I could pretend I was someone else so people would treat me like I was normal, too."

"But, Tyler, you're *not* normal. You're ten times *better* than normal. I think you're great. And I bet if your dad were here, he'd think you're pretty great, too. So if you still want to find him, I'll help you." It killed Clay to say it, but the kid deserved to find out for himself, no matter how disastrous it could end up. And hell, maybe

Tyler would be one of the lucky ones. Maybe Todd had learned to value others, especially his family....

No, that wasn't very likely.

"Nah," Tyler said. "I'm kinda over all that. I was looking at some stuff online and there was this blog that said it takes more than DNA to be a real dad. And I would rather have no dad at all then have some guy who ditches his family."

"I wish that when I was twenty, I knew half the stuff you know now. You are one smart kid."

"Smart enough that you'll let me look at that PC on the workshop counter over there?" Tyler said, hope filling his eyes.

"I'll tell you what, if you can fix that old PC, I'll buy you a jumbo cotton candy at the Fourth of July Festival."

Tyler smiled and stuck out his right hand. "A jumbo cotton candy *and* a new Geekon500 of my very own—and then you've got a deal."

From the moment Megan and the kids had unloaded their truck and begun to set up her display table at the festival, Tyler had started scanning the crowd, and she'd known who he'd been looking for.

Clay.

The boy hadn't stopped mentioning the man since they'd driven home from Lisa's game the other night. If she had to hear another word about the new computers Clay had donated to the school or how he'd promised Tyler that he could come into Zorba's a few times a week to help with repairs or about the new bleachers that were being erected at the community center gymnasium, she would scream.

Well, not really. She knew Clay was a generous man.

She didn't need her son, Caroline, Sally, the mayor and even the Franco sisters singing his praises every time she turned around, which they all had. But being a generous and an upstanding citizen didn't take away from the fact that he'd lied to her about who he was.

Unlike Todd, whose lies had masked a selfish, deceitful man, Clay's lies had masked a kind, generous heart.

But that didn't change the fact that he hadn't needed to lie to her or to perpetuate it more than a few days. He could have trusted her with his secret.

And worse, he'd seduced her while pretending to be someone else.

Megan had no more than set up her booth when Lisa asked for permission to play on the soccer field with a group of her friends. Since Megan knew the other mother overseeing the children, she agreed.

"Hey, Mom," Tyler said, "I'm going with the guys to walk around and check out some of the other booths. Okay?"

Megan looked around to see which guys Tyler was referring to and noticed a couple of boys she recognized from his summer enrichment program—one tall and overweight, the other thin and gangly like Tyler. They both looked as though they'd be more comfortable reading books and tapping away at laptops than they would be on the soccer field. And she realized that her son had finally found friends he could relate to, boys with the same interests he had.

She probably had Clay to thank for that, as well. Not only had he provided her son with bragging rights because he'd hung out with and worked with the world-famous computer entrepreneur Clay Jenkins, but he'd also helped boost Tyler's self-esteem.

Clay had been great with both of her children, as well as Pancho—and the kids were crazy about him.

Even if she were ready to forgive him, the fact remained that they were worlds apart, and that there could never be anything lasting between them.

It wasn't until later in the afternoon, when the kids were helping her dismantle her empty booth, that she gave up hope of seeing Clay. He clearly wasn't coming to the festival, and Megan was surprised that the knot of anger that had been cycling in her belly was being replaced with disappointment.

"Looks like you sold out again, Megan."

She recognized Don Carpenter's voice and turned in surprise to see him and his wife, Cindy, standing there holding a blanket.

"Hi, you two." She smiled warmly, glad to see the couple out and about around town. "You're both looking better and better each time I see you. How are you feeling?"

"Great. We just got back from a trip to San Antonio. Cindy finished her chemo, and the doctors are very optimistic. And I'm back to fighting weight." Don patted his ample belly. "In fact, my bride just told me it was high time I got back to the shop and stopped driving her crazy at home."

Megan laughed, but she envied the loving, caring glances that passed between the couple. That was what marriage was about. Being with someone who loved you and who would always look out for you, no matter what.

"It's good to hear that everything is getting back to normal." She didn't come out and say it, but with Don returning to work, that meant Clay would be leaving.

And the sooner he did, the quicker her broken heart would mend.

"It'll be better than normal," Don said. "Thanks to Geekon Enterprises, we won't have a single medical bill to pay—or any bills, for that matter. And the shop is now in better shape than ever."

"That's wonderful." And really, it was.

No one deserved it more than the Carpenters, and Megan had to acknowledge that if it weren't for Clay, things could have ended much, much worse.

Chalk up another point for the guy. He was definitely digging his way out of that deceitful hole he'd dug for himself. Well, not completely. But it wasn't nearly as deep as it once had been.

"Anyway, I'm happy you were able to make it to the festival, even though I think most of the vendors are winding down and closing up shop."

"That's okay," Don said. "We didn't come to buy anything. We came for the fireworks."

"That's right." Cindy slipped her arm through his. "We never miss them."

"Oh, but didn't you guys hear? They're not having the fireworks show this year."

"Actually, they weren't going to have them." Don lowered his voice to a whisper. "But an anonymous donor came through at the last minute, so the show is back on."

Lisa and Tyler, who'd just shoved the last empty crates into the back of the old farm truck Megan usually used only out on the orchard and at the farmers' market, shouted in unison, "Yes!"

"Can we go, Mom?" Lisa begged.

"Please." Tyler batted his eyes and clasped his hands.

Megan knew exactly who the donor had been. It couldn't have been anyone else. And it had been nice of Clay to do it, but if he wasn't careful, he'd have every charity case in East Texas shaking him down for favors.

Was that why he'd kept his identity a secret? To keep everyone from hitting him up for donations?

Megan hated to admit it, but she almost felt sorry for the guy.

"Okay, kids, let's get this stuff home and we'll come back for the fireworks."

"I wouldn't do that if I were you," Cindy said. "The parking lots are already full. They're having a concert in the park beforehand, and people brought picnic baskets and plan to stay. You should probably leave your truck here and get over to the park so you can find a good spot."

Megan thanked the Carpenters and sent them on their way. After securing everything in the truck, she dug around for one of the old quilts she used as a tablecloth from her booth display. She put Lisa in charge of finding the jackets and gave Tyler some cash to go over to the Kiwanis Club's food booth to buy them some homemade fried chicken and biscuits for a picnic dinner.

By the time they made it to the park, they had to step around a sea of blankets and folding chairs and small children before they could find a small square of grass to claim.

Megan sent the kids after lemonade from the stand with the smallest line while she unpacked their food. She'd just spread everything out when they returned— with an extra cup and an extra guest.

Clay.

"Look who's here," Lisa said, nearly spilling her lemonade in her excitement. "It's Mr. Johnson. I mean Peyton. I mean..." She bit down on her lip and gazed up at him. "What's your name again?"

"Maybe we should just all start over. Let me introduce myself. I'm Clay Jenkins. And I'd really like for you to call me Clay instead of Mr. Jenkins."

He looked better than ever, wearing jeans and boots and a dark blue T-shirt. She'd never seen him so casual before and if she hadn't known better, she'd think that he looked just like any other Brighton Valley local—one who was drop dead gorgeous, of course.

"Down in front," someone yelled at Clay, who was standing up, blocking the stage from the view of the people behind them.

"Please." Megan gestured toward the quilt. "Do you want to join us?"

"Thanks." As he knelt, she rearranged the food to make space for him.

"Here, Mom." Tyler handed her two cups. "Can you watch our drinks while we head over to see Mrs. Caroline and Sheriff Sam?"

"Don't you guys want to eat?" Megan asked, wishing they wouldn't leave her alone with the man who still made her pulse beat like crazy.

"Nah," Lisa said. "We had corn dogs earlier. And Mrs. Caroline said she and the sheriff would buy us cotton candy if we came and sat with them."

The kids took off running before Megan could even give them permission to go.

So that was the way of things. Her older friends had plotted to get her and Clay alone—and it had worked.

"I heard about your jam deal," Clay said. "Congratulations."

She'd told only the kids and Caroline, so she wasn't sure where he'd heard it. But that was what happened in small towns. People talked, and news spread like warm butter. "It was just an offer. And I really don't know any of the details yet."

If things were different, if Clay and she… Well, she'd love to take him to Dallas with her to that meeting. As it was, she'd have to go alone. Either way, she'd have an attorney look over the paperwork before she signed anything. She was a long way from having a "jam deal."

When it seemed as though there was nothing else to say—other than bringing up his big lie—she moved on to a safer topic. "The band is really good."

"Uh-huh." He shifted so that they were side by side and could both watch the lead singer.

"Almost too good," she added.

"What do you mean?"

"It's a classic-rock cover band. Normally, most of the bands that play at these local events are strictly country and western. Plus, I've never seen a band with this much talent play in Brighton Valley. It's almost as though someone with connections arranged for it.…" She let her comment hang in the air.

"What can I say? I've developed a strong hankering for classic-rock music. It reminds me of you."

Apparently, he'd also developed a hankering for using words like *hankering*.

She was touched by his gesture, but that didn't mean he planned to stick around.

He glanced her way, and the lift of her eyebrow must

have conveyed her doubts to him, because he reached for her hand.

She flinched from his touch, from the warmth, from the sizzle, but she didn't pull away.

"Seriously, Megan. I'm sorry for not telling you who I was sooner and I'm sorry that Todd 'A-hole' Redding was a jerk, and that he did a real number on you in the trust department."

"You're right about Todd. He came across as a nice guy, but he wasn't."

"I never thought of him as nice. Remember when I told you that I'd been bullied? Todd was the quarterback who made my life miserable in high school. So when I heard that he was your ex-husband, I was stunned—to say the least."

"Is that why you withdrew from me after we came home from Houston?"

"Yes, in part. And also because you told me how you felt about liars, when I was just about to confess that I'd deceived you. I'm not very good when it comes to communicating."

"I thought you regretted making love."

Clay reached for her hand. "Are you serious? Not for a single moment. I never regretted that."

So he hadn't been ready to ditch her, to toss her aside?

"I may have deceived you about my true identity, Megan. But I'm not a liar. And I'm not Todd. I love you. And I love the kids. I want us to be a family."

Now she was the one who was stunned. He loved her?

"Ever since the first day I arrived in town and saw you cleaning the apartment while singing that Fleetwood Mac song, I haven't been able to get you off my mind."

"You got all that from a Fleetwood Mac song?" Megan knew her response sounded silly, but he'd surprised her once again, and with her emotions buzzing, it was all she could get out.

"No, I got it from spending time with you and with the kids and with all the people in Brighton Valley. You made me look at my past and put that lonely and awkward geek to rest once and for all. You also made me look at my future and the fact that the only future I want is one with you and the kids in it."

"But what about Geekon and your business and your condo and your jets and all that? You can't really mean to give that all up just to move to some farm in Brighton Valley with us."

"First of all, it's not just some farm. It's where I want to be. Secondly, I'd give everything up if it meant I could be with you. There are some things that money can't buy—like love and a real home."

Megan's heart swelled to the breaking point, and tears welled in her eyes until they overflowed.

Clay cupped her face, and his thumbs brushed her cheeks, drying her tears. "I'm not going anywhere. And I'll wait forever, if that's what it takes, for you to realize that the man you see right now is the man that I really am—the man that I'll always be. And the man who loves you."

A loud pop sounded overhead and the sky lit up as people around them oohed and aahed. But Megan couldn't look at anything other than the man who was now kneeling before her.

"Marry me, Megan. I love you, and I'll spend every day of the rest of our lives proving it to you."

As the sky erupted in a blaze of brilliant sparks and bangs, Megan got to her knees and nodded yes. Then she wrapped her arms around Clay's neck. "I love you, too."

Then they kissed deeply and passionately for all of Brighton Valley to see—a bonus to the fireworks show.

When the display ended and the band started back up, laughter bubbled up inside her, bursting forth. She'd never been happier, freer to love and be loved.

"Besides," Clay said with the confidence of a man who had just won his woman's heart, "it's not like I'm giving up anything. In case you haven't noticed—" he nodded toward the band on stage "—I can afford to fly in almost everything I need right here to Brighton Valley."

"Hmm," she said. "What are you doing on Monday?"

"I can clear my calendar. What do you need?"

"I have my first business meeting in Dallas, and I'm a little nervous about going by myself. I'd like someone to sit with me. Not to do the negotiating, mind you. But to have my back and to make sure I don't give away the farm—so to speak."

"You bet, honey. I'll even fly you to Dallas. I'll be your coach or your executive assistant or your man Friday. Whatever you want, whatever you need, just say the word."

Before she could utter a response, Lisa and Tyler ran up to their blanket.

"Are you friends again?" Lisa asked. "Did you both say sorry and make up?"

"You don't kiss someone like that if you didn't," said Tyler.

"We're better than friends," Megan said.

"What's better than that?" Lisa asked.

Clay turned to the kids. "I just asked your mom to marry me. But I should ask how you guys feel about that, too, because I'd like to join your family—if you don't mind. And that would make me your stepfather."

"No way," Tyler said.

Megan turned to her son, who'd once thought Clay hung the moon. What was he possibly going to object to?

"We don't want you to be our stepdad," the boy said. "We want you to be our dad. And we want to be your kids."

Clay burst into a grin. "I can't think of anything I'd like more."

As the kids plopped down beside them, Megan threw her arms around Clay's neck and kissed him again with all the love in her heart, just as another boom went off, framing them with a colorful burst of fireworks.

Epilogue

It was a perfect day for an outdoor wedding, and no expense had been spared. Even the weather, which could be a little unpredictable in the fall, had cooperated, sending a nearly cloudless sky and temperatures in the mid-seventies.

A landscaper had laid sod last week near the orchard, where a party rental company had set up a gazebo, white covered chairs for the ceremony, and a bandstand, a dance floor, and tables and chairs for the reception. They'd also kept a florist and a caterer busy, as well as happy.

Megan, her mom and Zoe, who'd all worked hard on the decorations, were pleased with the way it had turned out. And so was Clay. He supposed you could say it had all the trappings for an elegant yet down-home wedding. And that it was where country charm met sophistication, which was good, because that was how their guest list read.

They'd invited his closest employees, like Zoe and others he wanted to be there. And then there were important business associates he thought they should include.

He didn't have any family, but Megan did—her three brothers, their wives and children, plus relatives of her stepfather, Darrel. There were also the Brighton Valley locals they couldn't leave out, like Sheriff Sam and Caroline; Sally the waitress; Mayor Ray Mendez and his wife, Catherine; Rick and Mallory Martinez; Hank and Marie Lazaro. Even the Franco sisters received an invitation.

They'd tried to keep the number down, but they'd still invited over two hundred people, and hardly anyone had declined.

Clay had surprised Megan's mother and stepfather by purchasing them a house in one of the new developments near Wexler, where they had RV parking for their motor home. Of course, the couple had been thrilled to hear of the wedding and to learn they'd be able to have the dream house they'd wanted but thought they could never afford on their fixed incomes.

They'd said they would start the long drive back to Brighton Valley, but Clay had told them not to bother. Instead he sent the corporate jet to pick them up in Yellowstone and bring them to Houston. Afterward he'd send them back the same way.

In the meantime, he'd offered to buy the farm from Megan's mother at more than the fair market price, which would provide her with a little nest egg.

Once the property was in Megan's name, she would

be able to expand the orchard and add any upgrades she wanted to the house. After the deal she'd made with Fowler Markets, she was going to need a bigger kitchen—industrial size, he suspected, because his soon-to-be wife had a better business head on her shoulders than he or the Fowler people had guessed.

She'd asked him to attend that meeting in early July, but she'd really needed only his moral support. In reality, she'd known her product and the value of it. And she'd held firm on the price and hadn't let them take advantage of her.

He did step in afterward and insist that she use his legal team to approve the contract before she signed it, and she'd been grateful for that.

She might refer to herself as a rube at times, just as he might think of himself as a geek—but they were both so much more than what met the eye. And together they made one hell of a team.

Now here they were, ready to start their lives together. Not just husband and wife but a family.

Dressed in a brand-new designer tuxedo, Clay stood near the gazebo, the orchard in the background. To his left, wearing a matching tuxedo, was his best man—and the only choice he possibly could make to take that position. Tyler had been thrilled to be asked and hadn't stopped grinning.

Clay suspected he was as happy to be getting a dad as Clay was to be getting a son.

As the music began, Lisa headed down the aisle wearing a peach-colored bridesmaid dress. It had taken her mother a lot of cajoling to get her to wear something "girlish," but once she'd agreed, the tomboy had actually gotten into the whole wedding thing. She'd even gone so far as to let the hairdresser style her hair just like her mother's.

The chords on the music shifted, and as the bridal march began, Megan started down the aisle between their seated guests.

If Clay had thought she was beautiful before, she was even more so today. Her cream-colored gown, a strapless vintage lace, fit her as though it had been made just for her. But then again, it had. Clay had asked Zoe to make sure she got exactly the gown she wanted, even if the designer had to make it personally.

Megan could have been a cover girl for a bridal magazine, with that mass of red curls piled up in an elegant swirl and a smile that turned Clay every which way but loose. His heart swelled to the point that he had to be standing an inch above the ground.

As Darrel Randall, Megan's stepfather, handed her off to him, her dazzling smile nearly struck him blind.

Fortunately, he'd asked Pastor Skinner to keep the ceremony short and sweet. And within minutes they were saying their vows.

"You may kiss the bride," the pastor said.

Clay took Megan in his arms and brushed his lips on hers. Had another kiss tasted as sweet? Had another promise meant so much?

When it was over, they turned to face their guests, and Pastor Skinner said, "May I be the first to introduce you to Mr. and Mrs. Clay Jenkins."

Their guests, all 217 of them, clapped and cheered as Clay led his bride down the aisle to start their new lives as man and wife.

"I love you," she said. "You've made me the happiest woman in the world."

"Not as happy as you and the kids have made me." Then he bent and kissed her softly yet thoroughly, letting her know that the geek in him had merged into the man—and that he'd finally found the one place in the world where he truly belonged now and forever.

* * * * *

A sneaky peek at next month...

Cherish™

EXPERIENCE THE ULTIMATE RUSH OF FALLING IN LOVE

My wish list for next month's titles...

In stores from 18th July 2014:

☐ The Rebel and the Heiress – Michelle Douglas

& A Cowboy's Heart – Rebecca Winters

☐ Not Just a Convenient Marriage – Lucy Gordon

& The Billionaire's Nanny – Melissa McClone

In stores from 1st August 2014:

☐ A Wife for One Year – Brenda Harlen

& From Maverick to Daddy – Teresa Southwick

☐ A Groom Worth Waiting For – Sophie Pembroke

& Crown Prince, Pregnant Bride – Kate Hardy

Available at WHSmith, Tesco, Asda, Eason, Amazon and Apple

Just can't wait?

0714/23

Special Offers

Every month we put together collections and longer reads written by your favourite authors.

Here are some of next month's highlights— and don't miss our fabulous discount online!

On sale 18th July

On sale 18th July

On sale 18th July

The World of Mills & Boon

There's a Mills & Boon® series that's perfect for you. There are ten different series to choose from and new titles every month, so whether you're looking for glamorous seduction, Regency rakes, homespun heroes or sizzling erotica, we'll give you plenty of inspiration for your next read.

By Request

Relive the romance with the best of the best
12 stories every month

Cherish™

Experience the ultimate rush of falling in love.
12 new stories every month

INTRIGUE...

A seductive combination of danger and desire...
7 new stories every month

Desire™

Passionate and dramatic love stories
6 new stories every month

nocturne™

An exhilarating underworld of dark desires
3 new stories every month

For exclusive member offers go to
millsandboon.co.uk/subscribe